# THE BRILLIANT MIRAGE: A NOVEL

NADIJA MUJAGIC

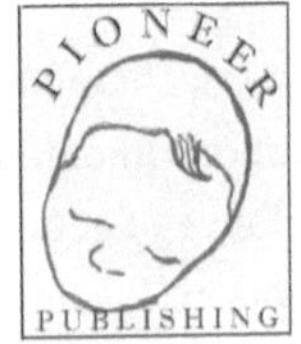

# PROLOGUE

For a hundredth time already, Oscar Gonzales slammed the telephone receiver and yelled out "Damn it! Why the hell is he not picking up?"

His wife came out of the kitchen with rubber gloves up to her elbows, covered with bubbles from the dish soap. Wide-eyed, she stood between the kitchen and the living room and looked at Oscar, astounded by his scream. He was sitting on the couch, his face buried in his hands, his feet apart, motionless.

"Everything okay?" Lauren sounded frightened, eagerly waiting for Oscar to say something. He unburied his face from his hands and shot a gaze in her direction.

He saw Lauren standing there in her apron and

gloves. Her dark hair turned wet and flat on the top from the sweat produced above the kitchen sink, her make-up oozed on the side, and the worried look on her face made her unsightly.

"Everything is okay." Oscar forced a smile. He hated it when his wife worried. It was in her nature to be concerned about every little thing, but Oscar tried to curtail it. "It's just that Carl isn't picking up the phone again."

She tilted her head and placed empathy on her face. "Oh, dear. You really do care about your friend so much."

"Well, yeah, I've known him all my life. I know you think he's weird, but I can't just ignore him, you know." Lauren took off the gloves, revealing her skinny and graceful arms. Even though she was in her fifties, her skin looked as smooth as milk. Since they didn't have children, albeit against their own wishes,

Lauren had plenty of time and reason to take good care of both of them.

She approached Oscar and sat down next to him, placing her hand on his knee.

"You have a big heart, my love. This is why I married you." She smiled like an angel. "Yes, I think he's weird, but there is a good reason for it, don't you think?"

"I suppose." Oscar paused to think, staring at a

spot in front of him, and said, "I could never figure out the guy. I thought I knew him better, since I've known him all my life." He looked at Lauren and she smiled at him again.

"It's nice that you care about him. So sweet."

"Listen, I think I need to make a trip to his place today. I'm worried about him."

"Of course," Lauren said like it was a no brainer. "And bring him a plate of food I made yesterday." She jumped from the couch and headed for the kitchen.

Oscar shook his head, reflecting on his last encounter with his friend Carl Walker. That was about two months ago. He did the same thing he was doing now, not answering many of his calls and then convincing him later everything was okay. When Oscar arrived at his place that last time, it looked messy and disheveled, like it hadn't been cleaned in months. Carl kept telling him everything was okay, but Oscar suspected that this couldn't be farther from the truth. But Carl didn't share much. Ever since his wife died, he seemed a bit estranged, like he was coping with the loss and loneliness on his own terms.

And now, here they were again.

Lauren came out of the kitchen holding a bag with a plate inside. "Hold it straight up, honey. The food might spill over otherwise."

"Okay, sweetheart." Oscar gave her a kiss on the forehead and went to use the bathroom once again before he hit the road. An hour ride from New Hampshire to Massachusetts sometimes turned much longer with unexpected accidents along the way.

He grabbed the food, kissed Lauren on the cheek, and headed through the door. "I'll be back in a few hours."

"Okay, honey. Drive safe. And say hi to Carl. Hopefully he remembers me."

Oscar paused for a second and looked at his wife, wondering why she'd say something like that. Of course, he would remember her. Why wouldn't he? Carl was strange, but not out of his mind.

When Oscar arrived at Carl's building, an elderly lady opened the building door and he snuck into the building behind her. He smiled at her and she looked at him suspiciously, though she didn't say a word. When Oscar came up to Carl's door, he knocked.

He brought his ear closer to the door, and he heard a radio at a low volume and Carl talking. Who was he talking to? Carl didn't get to socialize much. This was particularly the case since his wife died.

When Oscar realized Carl wasn't coming to the door, he knocked again. Nothing.

"Carl, open the door."

"Who is it?" A cracked voice emerged on the other side of the door.

"It's me, Oscar. I tried to call you several times in the past few days and you never answer my phone calls. Are you all right?"

He felt Carl's eye resting on the peephole and watching him grow impatient as he rolled his eyes and clenched his fists. Carl's voice came much closer and clearer.

"Yes, Oscar. I'm alright. You can leave now."

Oscar felt Carl didn't appreciate this commotion or disturbance coming from him. He'd told him a million times already that he was okay, and he didn't need to worry if he didn't pick up his phone. But Oscar insisted that something could be wrong. It was in his nature to care for his friends, for the people he loved.

Oscar was about to say something until Carl said, "Oscar, are you alone right now?"

"Yeah, why?"

"Oscar, if you want us to remain friends, you need to be truthful with me."

"What? I'm being truthful with you, Carl. There's no one standing next to me right now. I'm all alone.

Why don't you open the door and see it for yourself?"

"I'm pretty sure I saw an arm moving next to you. Who is it?"

What was with paranoia, Oscar wondered. "Carl. Please. Let's not do this."

"Do what?" Carl sounded confused. "Stop making up stuff. And open the door." "Tell me who you're with."

"Carl!" Oscar's impatience kept growing. Carl cracked the door open with the door chain keeping it locked. He could now see the whole of Oscar: his baggy pants, his over-worn shoes, his body charged with concern as if he was about to be electrocuted. He saw a slice of Carl's face protruding behind the door and offered a smile. "Hi, Carl."

"What can I do for you, Oscar?" Carl changed the angle of his head as if to see who was standing beside Oscar, but the space was void of any other persons.

"I came here to see you. May I come in?"

Carl removed the chain from the door and opened it. "Come in."

Oscar entered his apartment and hugged his friend. He moved away but still had his arms on Carl's. "I'm here for you if you need anything."

"That's good to hear, but I think I'm all set." Oscar nodded and looked Carl in the eye. "Okay, Carl, okay. Everything will be fine. I'm here if you ever need anything."

Carl just stood there not saying a word. The day was rainy and raw, and he finally said he could use a nice warm shower. He added, "Oscar, I have important things to do here, you shouldn't disturb me like this."

"What important things?" Oscar's voice was high-pitched. It surprised him to hear his friend occupied himself with activities.

Carl put his hands on his hips and spat out, "Really, Oscar?"

"I... I did not know you had a busy life, that's all." "Oscar, I just came back from Germany, it's been

a long trip. I need to rest."

"Germany? You never told me you were going to Germany." Oscar looked around the apartment to find luggage lying around or any evidence of Carl's recent travel, but nothing of that nature was in his sight. He couldn't help but wonder how his friend traveled in his frail state. Carl could barely walk.

"Do I need to tell you everything?" They paused and looked at each other, both with surprise on their face.

"How... how did you get there?" "On a plane. Duh!"

Oscar stood there and watched Carl's eyes scan his apartment; he could sense that he was an unwelcome guest today. But a lot of questions lingered in his mind, and he didn't know where to begin.

"What did you do in Germany?"

Carl turned around and walked in the opposite

direction. He waved his arm like it was no big deal. "I had some business there. It's a long story." He sat down on his couch and crossed his leg over the other.

"Oh." Oscar was curious now. He thought he knew his friend well, but his doubts were growing by the second. "Maybe you can tell me when you go on a trip next time. What do you think of that?"

Carl waved his arm again like it was no big deal. He sighed and looked at Oscar straight up. He forced a smile as if to show his pleasure with the adventure, but also to conceal something unspoken, and said, "It was... it was quite a trip."

# PART I

**1**

———

I have never been the best at anything. Some people are best at something, like juggling and eating at the same time, some are best at singing and playing a musical instrument also at the same time, some possess special skills that no one else does. But me? I've been mediocre at pretty much everything I have touched upon in life. The only thing I might be considered best at—though it's not even considered a skill—is constantly walking, putting in at least ten miles a day. I'd walk everywhere: around my apartment, in the neighborhood, around my office... I wasn't much of a chatter. When I ran into somebody, I wouldn't stop to talk with them. I'd keep walking and I would hear their voice behind me inquiring: how are you? How's your day going? Nice weather today, eh? I'd yell out responses as I kept walking. They wouldn't tell me this, but I heard a colleague whisper one day, saying "Walkie Talkie" followed by a chuckle. I wasn't offended by the nickname, because the name was fitting.

For sure, I had dromomania. When I told people that this was the case, they'd all ask me: what is dromomania? They could look it up, yes, but they seemed quite curious and wanted their question answered immediately. Dromomania, my friend, is an uncontrollable desire to travel or walk in my case. No, it had nothing to do with my last name—Walker —although many suspected that might be the case. When I was younger, I traveled a lot on a whim: one year, I'd pack my bag and fly over to Europe, randomly choosing countries I wanted to visit. Another year, I road tripped and drove from Massachusetts until I reached California. It was easy in the day, when taking a vacation or sabbatical from work still secured you a job when you returned from your adventures. When I got married, I put my travels on pause, as my new bride detested flying and was afraid of it. We tried to work on the problem, but every time she even had a thought about flying, she'd trembled and produced an inconsiderable amount of sweat. We retired from the travel idea altogether, and that was when my body itched to walk constantly.

Now that I am aged and widowed—though I

don't consider myself that old—I'd roam on the streets of my town, rain or shine, for hours. I'd stop by my favorite convenience store on the corner of Main and Adams Street, buy a bottle of Pepsi to quench my thirst and continue walking.

A new opportunity to travel and walk arrived one day unexpectedly, like a storm breaking out on a sunny day.

But my lucky chance begun on a rainy day in September. Specifically, when I ran into my neighbor Drew Trollope. We both lived in a two-story building made of red brick—one of many on our street, which wasn't so uncommon for our town in Massachusetts. It was a brand-new building with luxurious amenities, a pool in the back of the building and a tennis court on the side. My apartment had a dishwasher and a sink disposal, which was a huge upgrade from my previous home and, needless to say, they helped save time.

There were about thirty-four apartments in total spread around the building. Mostly, I kept to myself and didn't know many of our neighbors. Drew Trollope was one of the few people I got to know because he was our mailman. He was in his forties, single, never married and, if I may be crude, not so good-looking. He was about six feet tall, skinny, his teeth were yellow, a nose sharp and long, and oily hair combed to one side. If he weren't so friendly every time I ran into him, I'd probably try to avoid talking to him or making his acquaintance. But as it were, we'd chat about the weather and he'd ask me if I watched the Sox games the night before. Typical small talk.

That day in September, I saw him in the building lobby. He seemed a bit rattled or nervous, and I couldn't put my finger on why. I looked around to find the culprit of his concerns, but there was nothing in our surrounding that I thought would prompt him to look wide-eyed and shaky.

"Hey, Carl," he whispered. "I have something to tell you."

"Hey, Drew." I tried to stay cool and nonchalant about his erratic behavior. "Yeah, go ahead. Tell me."

"Carl, I can't do it here." He looked around as if some invisible person were chasing him.

"Okay. Well…"

He cut me off. "Let's go to my apartment, Carl."

"Your… your apartment?" I couldn't recall the last time I had visited someone's home. By then, I assumed I had forgotten the guest-visiting etiquette.

"Yeah. I need privacy, Carl. I can't say it here. Let's go. Follow me." When he moved swiftly, I followed him as if he had some strong gravity force that pulled me in. It was probably my curious nature that needed to discover what Drew had to say. And I was hoping it was going to be good and juicy.

As we walked up the stairs, he was in front of me. I noticed his slacks wrinkled along the entire length of his legs—they were too big for his stature. His shirt was untucked, and it covered his rear. His vest had a hole in the left bottom corner, but I assumed he either never noticed it or he didn't care. As we walked, a trail of the ramen noodle smell attached to Drew engulfed me. I tried to not breathe, as it was making me nauseous. The sound of his shoe soles scraping against the stairs echoed along the building, and I couldn't wait to arrive at his apartment at last.

When we stepped in front of his apartment door, he pulled out a keychain with a multitude of keys that made him look like a dungeon master. They rattled and shook, making an incredible noise. Why so many keys? I wondered. But then I reminded myself that as a postman, he probably had a lot of mailboxes to unlock and open. He delivered mail to our building, and he once told me he knew every single person's name off the top of his head here. The issue was that he didn't know what they looked like, so they mainly remained ungreeted and ignored.

He looked through the key chain to locate the one for his apartment door. The rattling noise kept filling the silence. He must have been still nervous as he rummaged through the key chain. I stared at his bald spot on the back of his head, partially covered by the oily hair. Finally, the door opened up. Drew crossed the door threshold and turned around to greet me in his apartment.

"Come in." He continued to whisper. I thought maybe he had someone at home visiting and taking a nap, but as I looked around, the apartment seemed empty. It amassed untasteful furniture and a bunch of other junk sitting on the floor. The stench was unbearable. I couldn't tell what it was, but I took the liberty to come to the closest window and open it or else I would have vomited right there on the floor. When I opened the window, the level of noise in the room increased from the children playing and bicycling outside. School had just started, and the children must have wanted to take advantage of the pleasant weather before they hunkered down in the winter.

I turned around to see Drew sitting on his worn-out couch. He pulled a cigarette pack from his rear pocket, shoved a cigarette in his mouth, and lit it. He inhaled the cigarette smoke like he was about to experience nirvana. The exhale seemed long, and the smoke kept coming out of his mouth, forming a stinky cloud between us.

"Sit down, Carl." His voice sounded calmer. He no longer whispered.

I looked around and only then noticed a chair

sitting across from the couch. The backrest was hidden by several shirts and jackets, and the seat was covered with a pile of mail secured with long rubber bands. I winced when I noticed the pile, because someone out there could be anxiously waiting for a piece of mail sitting in this very same pile.

He noticed the sign of my distress and offered a smile. "Don't worry. It's today's mail. I will make rounds first thing tomorrow morning."

"Oh good. I was slightly worried." He lifted his arm and moved it like I shouldn't care. I removed the pile from the chair and sat down, facing Drew head on. He seemed to enjoy his cigarette, as he inhaled smoke as soon as he exhaled it. I sat in the chair and watched him. A whole minute passed, and I was growing awkward. My leg shook, vibrating my entire body. Drew pulled out the cigarette pack quickly again to offer me a cigarette, but I shook my head.

"No, thanks." Smoking didn't go well with walking. I'd tried before.

"Carl, I have something to tell you," he said.

"Yes, I know." I looked him straight in the eye, and even he noticed I was losing my patience. "That's why we're both here."

"Right, right. Listen. I brought you here to tell you a secret no one knows." I kept staring at him without saying a word. His eyes twinkled like stars, and he seemed to have transformed into a young boy about to play with his favorite toy. "I discovered yesterday that there's a secret underground place. No one has had access to it yet. Apparently, only a few people in the world know where it's located."

He inhaled and exhaled the smoke again. This time, I said nothing because I tried to absorb the information he just shared.

"A secret underground place?" I repeated to make sure I heard him correctly.

"Yes, Carl. A secret underground place." I laughed. Drew now stared at me and patiently waited for my laughter to subdue.

"Alrighty then." I would not take the bait. Now I was growing concerned that our mailman was simply batshit crazy.

"You listen to me, Carl. This is for real. The only person close to us who knows the location of this place lives in this building."

"Oh." This was getting better and better by the second.

"Her name is Ursula, and she lives three doors down from me." Until then, I had not heard of Ursula. But then again, I didn't know almost any of my neighbors except for Drew. And I regretted that a little. Regardless of my growing suspicion, I wanted to find out where this conversation was going.

"A-ha. Okay."

"Ursula is a woman in her eighties who moved

from Germany when World War II ended. She worked for the Nazis as a secretary, but she kept incognito mostly. I heard she wanted to flee during the war, but she had no place to go, so she kept working for the Nazis, pretending she enjoyed it."

He flicked his cigarette in the ashtray, missing it so the ash was everywhere on the table.

"The underground place was a big secret during the war, of course. It's where they hid things, apparently. I hear Ursula was told about the place when she became an essential employee."

"An essential employee?" Drew's choice of words didn't sit well. "Is that what they called them back in the day?"

"Well, shit, I don't know. But I heard they forced her to move about. During the Wannsee conference, she was sitting in the same room with all the officials planning the genocide. The conference started at ten thirty, and by the time they came up with the extermination plan, it was already noon."

"Wait, it took them only an hour and a half to plan the genocide?"

"Sure did. Someone later found the meeting minutes from the conference. The language was obscure and didn't include those red flag words, but it's all there. And Ursula was the one to take those notes."

I looked at Drew, remaining silent. I tried to

process what he was telling me. My crossed leg felt numb, so I slowly picked it up with both hands and placed it on the chair. When my leg felt numb, it signaled that I had to walk wherever my legs would take me. My inner wish at the moment was for Drew to finish the story. I did not know where he was going with it.

"Here's the most important part that might interest you." He closed his eyes for a second, as if he was trying to concentrate on his words. "The underground secret place had got diamonds hidden inside. Before the Nazis capitulated, an army officer went there and dropped a bag full of ice. Ursula was there with him when he did it."

My leg returned to feeling normal. "Why should all this concern me?"

"It should concern you if you want to help me find those diamonds. Ursula might be the only person in the world who knows where those diamonds are there."

"Uh-huh." As I was saying this, I felt my right brow raise. "Go on."

"Now, here's the problem with Ursula. Actually, a couple of problems with Ursula." Drew leaned forward and pursed his lips like he was about to spit on my face. "Ursula has dementia and can't recall almost anything about her past."

Drew inhaled cigarette smoke and tilted his head backward to release the smoke into the ceiling.

"Apparently, she has children who live out of the state and visit her on rare occasions. I've seen people in scrubs come into our building and head for the second floor. I assume they go visit her."

I looked at Drew and still waited for the punch line. For one, I was unclear why he was telling all this to me. Did he not have any friends?

"What's the other crazy thing about Ursula, if I may ask?"

"Oh. I guess it's not so crazy as it is inconvenient. She's an old cranky lady. She's not approachable. I've heard some stories."

"Drew, why are you telling me all this?"

Drew widened his eyes as if he just saw a ghost.

"Why?" He shook his head. "If it isn't so obvious. I'm asking for your help to get Ursula to recall the secret location, so we can go get the diamonds. The diamonds are just sitting there, waiting to be discovered."

"And you want to be the one to discover them?" I asked, and a second later, hoped he wouldn't sense the sarcasm in my voice. Drew didn't quite strike me as an adventurous type capable of untangling or digging into the past.

"Yes. With your help." His grin was as large as a house. The cigarette was burned to the butt, and he placed it in the ashtray, swirling it around while he looked me right in the eye.

"Me? Why me, Drew?" Now I was feeling uneasy, because Drew and I barely knew each other, and now he wanted to plan a high-end operation that I'd only seen in action movies.

"Why not you? I've seen you walk. You've got the energy of five bulls." His conspicuous grin returned, and his yellow teeth were protruding from his gums. "Plus, you're retired now and have more time on your hands. I'm a mailman and can't quit my job. They need me, Carl."

I rolled my eyes. "Sure, I get it, but I'm no Sean Connery, you know. And this is not a movie."

"Sure, sure. But this underground place does exist, and those diamonds are hidden there. If you or me don't find 'em, someone else will."

Drew stood up and went to the kitchen. I could no longer see him, but I heard him rummaging through the dishes. Just by the sound of it, I could tell his kitchen cabinets were disorganized and uninviting. I heard the sink pipe run with water, then close, and Drew slurping. A few seconds later, he appeared behind the kitchen wall separating his delusions and me, and he screeched like he was performing on Broadway.

"So?! What do you say? You wanna do it?"

I let the sound of the children from the outside

break the discomfort in the room. I twiddled my thumbs and looked at Drew, realizing how completely immersed and mesmerized I was by this conversation. No one had told me a story like this before. A story that seemed unusual and far-fetched, but I had a lot of time on my hands, and I was willing to listen.

"What exactly do you want from me?"

Drew took a few steps forward and patted the back pocket to get his cigarettes out. He lit another one, inhaled and exhaled the smoke, and sat down on the couch. "Since you're a busy bee walking all the time, maybe you can travel to the roads once we find out where they are?" He shrugged his shoulders. "I'm a mailman. I travel from building to building, and that's my life."

I felt sad for Drew. He was in his early forties, but in that moment, he seemed like an old man whose life was adrift. I had barely known Drew, but that familiar exasperated look on his face made me feel I had known him for ages.

"Listen, Drew," I said, trying to choose the right words so as not to hurt his feelings. "I don't know if I'm the right person for this mission. But to be fair, I'll give it some thought and see how I feel about it in a day or two."

He looked at me and exhaled. "Okay."

I stood up, ready to go, since my leg was about to get numb again.

"Wait, wait." Drew lifted his arm, and I faced his palm near my face. "One more thing. I've noticed a young guy deliver groceries to Ursula every other day. I'm going to knock on her door tomorrow to see if she needs help with anything else. You want to come?"

I waved my hand as I moved a step ahead toward the front door. "No, thanks. But good luck with that."

With those words, I exited through the door and ran to the street. The familiar path drew me into its vastness, and my feet were moving with rapidness. A child with a bicycle nearly hit me; he was around six and was learning to balance on his bike. The conversation with Drew threw me off a bit. When I walk, I look at things, observe the people, and that's all that existed—people in particular: I'd check out their sizes and shapes, their facial expressions (usually worried looking), whether they moved slowly or quickly, I wonder about their final destination and try to guess what their family history is: are they solo or married, do they have children, are they happy with their familial life or does the sudden change of pace seem burdensome and boring? But this time, I wandered on the streets like I was possessed. I paid no attention to anything or anyone. Each street looked the same. Each street corner was like a spitting image of the previous one. I had no sense of time. Time was lost on me, and I did not know how far I reached until I walked to the infamous large brick building that has been abandoned for years. For the first time, I didn't bother to wonder why the building was abandoned or who owned it. For the first time, it just looked like a stack of bricks waiting for a new owner to revive it.

Drew got me. I was out of sorts. But it was quite possible that just being in contact with another human got me all awry.

When I arrived home, it was already dark and fall temperatures crept into homes. A photograph of my young wife greeted me in the hallway. It had been a decade since she passed. I paused for a second to catch a breath and then took the photograph of my wife to bring her closer to my face. I blew her a kiss goodnight and went to bed, thinking about what a strange day was behind me.

**2**

———

I woke up groggy from the dreams that night. In my dreams, my wife turned into a hyena and she was laughing at me, about to attack me. I ran through the tall grass in a jungle and I kept feeling afraid the hangry animal would catch me. Just as the hyena grabbed me, her teeth about to bite into my neck, I screamed. Lately, all my dreams were blurring with reality. Not the hyena dream, but the other ones. I couldn't discern if certain things really happened to me in a parallel dimension or in my previous life, if I ever had one, if I dreamt them, or if I saw them in a movie a while ago. Some scenes resurfaced in my head, leading me to ponder whether they were real. Having a wife was not questioned. A wife I was pretty sure I had. But she looked nothing like a hyena.

A doubt cast over me on whether I ever had a conversation with Drew about hidden diamonds. I wanted to believe so badly that it didn't happen, because I couldn't see myself getting into the adventure of hunting for diamonds. I wasn't the man for him, even though he believed I could find the place and unearth the ice. Everything was so obscure.

I closed my eyes and pictured Drew in his wrinkled slacks, a vest over a shirt, smoking a cigarette and telling me about Ursula, our neighbor, and the secret place where diamonds were hidden. His image looked pretty clear, as if he was sitting across from me all over again, smiling with his yellow teeth protruding from his gums. Yes, Drew's story was coming to life again, and it hit me I wasn't dreaming after all. I opened my eyes and shook my head, realizing my silly predicament.

I got up from my bed and went to the bathroom to wash my face. When I bent down to the sink, I heard someone knocking on my door. Who could it be this early in the morning? I walked outside the bathroom and the grandfather clock in the hallway showed ten in the morning. Holy shit, ten am. I couldn't remember the last time I slept in so late. I opened the door, and on the doormat stood Drew. He was wearing his postal uniform and most likely getting ready to do his delivery rounds. I couldn't tell if he was pissed, sad, or desperate looking. I wasn't fully awake, but I suspected why Drew was paying me a visit and standing in front of my front door.

Ever since he told me about the underground place with diamonds, I tried to avoid Drew like a plague. I knew the approximate time he delivered our mail, so I made sure to be outside for a walk around that time. My attempt to tell him it was probably all an old wives' tale was what I thought about all of that. But I had no heart to shatter his dreams or be an outright asshole.

"Hey, Drew."

"Hey, Carl."

"What... what can I do for you?"

"You know why I'm here, Carl. Don't pretend like you're clueless." Drew whispered so that none of our neighbors could listen in. The walls were sometimes as thin as paper.

"You wanna come in?" I didn't really want him to be in my apartment, but that was the best I could do, considering I ignored him for so long. It had been almost a month since he broke the news about the underground place and asked for my help.

"No. But I will." He entered my apartment slowly and then stood in the hallway like a sad statue.

I walked to the living room and told him to follow me. He came into my living room and pulled a pack of smokes out of his back pocket.

"If you don't mind. No smoking, please." If he only knew how much I detested cigarette smoke.

"Seriously?"

"Yeah, this is a non-smoking home." I raised my voice a bit, and Drew seemed to have noticed my annoyance. "Okay, Drew, speak up." I was losing my patience. My usual morning routine was to put a kettle on the stove and make some tea, but Drew disrupted my flow. He needed to get it out fast.

"Why are you leaving me hanging, Carl?" He looked like a little puppy with drooping eyes. "Why can't you tell me if you're in or not?"

I tilted my head slightly, and of course, I knew the answer to his question. I waited for this moment to come. He would seek me out again and ask about a treasure hunt.

"Well, let me tell you why, Drew. There's no real evidence the secret underground place exists. There's no real evidence that they stashed diamonds in a corner of such a place. There's no way you're gonna have Ursula tell us her secrets. Especially if she's an old cranky lady, like you said. I'll tell you like it is: I don't want to waste my time searching for something that may not exist. I'd rather stay home and do what I usually do."

"What? Walk like a crazy maniac?"

"Hey, hey, hey. Easy with insults. If you want to catch flies, you better turn that vinegar into honey."

"Yes, sorry, Carl," he said. "I brought you this." I noticed only then that he was holding my paper, the Boston Globe, in his hand when he extended his arm. "I saw it in the lobby downstairs."

"Ah thanks." I grabbed the newspaper and, in my mind, I pictured myself sitting in my favorite café and poring over the news. I softened my voice a bit when I asked him this question: "Did I make myself clear?"

"You sure did. I'm afraid you're going to regret it someday." With that, Drew turned around and hurried out of my apartment. Don't slam the door, don't slam the door, don't slam the door. The door slammed. Son of a gun!

I made my tea and got myself ready to go for the usual morning visit at the café around the corner. The day was crisp. It was October 19, 1987. The leaves were nearly gone from the nearby trees, making holes as I looked up at the sky. My steps were deliberate and fast toward the café. It took only several minutes to find myself in front of it. When I looked through the window, the place looked deserted and dark. Was it closed? What was happening? But then I saw the movement inside, and I was happy to discover the place was open.

I entered, but the usual vibe greeted me. Anna, the café barista of many years, stood behind the counter. Every time she saw me, she'd exclaim my name like she'd seen Jesus.

"Carl! Good morning!"

"Good morning, Anna."

"The usual?"

"Yeah, sure, the usual." She pulled a raisin muffin out of the glass box and handed it to me. Sometimes she'd forget to charge me, so I'd pay her right away. Her big brown eyes would look at me with glee, and I couldn't help but leave her a big tip in the tip jar.

"Thank you, Carl." She'd run a hand over her short blonde hair, like a nervous gesture, and smile. If she were older, maybe I would ask her out on a date. But frankly, I wasn't entirely sure if she liked me for me or if she exhibited customer service the same way with everyone. I also wondered what she might have thought of me, given my daily carefree visits. A fit guy in his early fifties who paid a visit to the coffee shop every single day. She must have wondered, at least once, I'd imagine, why I wasn't at work or, if I didn't work, how I sustained my well-being. Was I rich? Did I inherit lots of money once upon a time from an abusive, rich father of mine? Did I ever work?

If I ever took her out on a date, I'd tell her I made a lot of money on stock investments. I was so good at buying the right stock all the time, like some little bird whispered in my ear, telling me the right choice. And then, months later, the value of these stocks would grow, making me rich and happy. I made so much money that I quit my job and retire early. Would Anna be happy to hear this? What kind of man did she desire? Maybe she was already taken. I wasn't much into the dating scene, anyway. Not since my wife had passed. I'd still feel like I was cheating on her, even though she must have turned into worm food by now.

Anna looked at me with her flirty smile and told me to shout out if I needed anything else. I resorted to my usual corner and opened up today's newspaper. My heart pounded when I saw the headline on the first page in big black letters:

STOCKS CRASH BY 508 POINTS, A SIGNIFICANT DECREASE
COULD THIS BE 1929 ALL OVER AGAIN?

I stopped in my tracks and reread it a few times. Stocks plunge, stocks plunge, stocks plunge... Was I no longer rich? It was the first thought that crossed my mind and cut my belly like a sharp knife.

I continued reading:

*Stock market prices plunged yesterday, giving Wall Street*

*its worst day in history of stock trading and raising fears of recession.*

*As stock prices plummeted, several economists foresee that 1987 could very well look like 1929. Unless the stock market bounces back quickly and substantially, most Americans are likely to be hurt by the dramatic decline in the stock values, even those who do not own stocks at all.*

My life might change in an instant. What if the stock's price continued to plummet? Would I need to readjust my life? Find a job? Would I need to forego my endless walks and morning trips to the coffee shop? I liked my daily routine. I was happy and content with my life as it was.

I looked up from the newspaper and closed my eyes. The sound of the coffee machine seemed to get louder. Anna was humming a tune; if I told her about what I just read, I wondered if she'd understand. I opened my eyes, and the coffee shop looked as if it was wrapped up in a white cloud. I was feeling dizzy and disoriented. Maybe that was why.

I flipped through the pages slowly, but I wasn't paying close attention to any of the words. Then, suddenly, like a boxing glove about to make a jab at me, another headline popped up:

### German Diamonds Still Missing
#### Munich, Germany
#### October 19, 1987

*In the most recent archived documents generated under the Nazi rule, it is believed that over five hundred 2-carat diamonds went missing upon the war's end. Wide speculations as to the diamonds' location are still being made. When the war ended, the diamonds were in the possession of a German general whose name was withheld in the documents. It is believed that he was captured shortly after the war ended, making him the only person knowing the whereabouts of such diamonds. The value of the stones is estimated at two million US dollars.*

MY HEARTBEAT SKIPPED AGAIN. I stood up like a torpedo and headed for the door. I heard Anna's voice in the background. "Bye, Carl, see you tomorrow!" But my body automatically kept going. I walked so fast, I was afraid I'd trip and fall. The cold air was hitting my face, and my nose started to run.

Many possibilities crossed my mind: diamonds. They were a future. If Drew and I got a hold of them, they would erase all my troubles. I'd keep living my comfortable retired life. I'd never worry if stocks plunge again or make me a broke man. It didn't matter anymore. I was on a mission—I had to find the diamonds, what seemed to be my ticket to a comfortable life.

As I cut through the crispness of the air, there was only one destination I had in mind. The only place I wanted to reach as quickly as humanly possible: Drew's place.

I knocked on his door frantically, like a lunatic. He didn't open immediately, so I banged on his door again. Just as my hand was about to hit the door for the third time, the door opened up.

"What on earth?" Drew's face looked angry.

"I will do it," I blurted out. Drew looked to his right and then his left down the hall, and signaled for me to come in. We both now stood in his smelly apartment. He took a cigarette pack out of his pocket and lit it in his mouth.

"You always change your mind so fast?" He lifted his hand, holding the cigarette.

"Don't mess with me, Drew. Don't think you have an upper hand here. You need me just as much as I need you."

"Yeah. yeah." Drew smiled. For the first time, I saw a potential of this man being charming and handsome. Or, at least I wanted to believe that as I pictured him becoming my partner in the hunt.

"What's next? Let's think about it." I cut to the chase.

"Well, our first step is to tame that cranky old

bitch." I let out a loud laugh. I didn't know why, but that sounded extra funny at the moment. "We need to go see her as often as possible, make ourselves friendly and available. And then somehow get a lot of info out of her... if she can remember anything."

"Does she have any of her family members? Do you know?"

He inhaled cigarette smoke and flipped the ash into the tray. He shook his head. "Doesn't look like it."

"Oh good. I suppose it will make it easier for us to get closer to her," I retorted, like I just discovered another planet. "When do we start?"

"I have to make delivery rounds today, but I have a day off tomorrow. How about tomorrow?"

"That works." My answer spat out like a bullet flying out of a pistol. Seriously. What else was I going to do? For a second, I was afraid I seemed too eager, but I didn't care. I was determined to go on with the plan and see it through. "How should we do this? What's the plan?"

"Relax." Drew smiled like he had been on a similar mission a million times before. "Just follow me. Don't say much tomorrow, okay? I'm a mailman. I know how to deal with people." And with that, he inhaled cigarette smoke and shortly after disappeared into the thick stinking cloud. For me, it was the first time to hear that mailmen were people pleasers.

"When we find the diamonds, we split them fifty-fifty?" I wanted to make the terms clear up front.

"Oh, Carl. That's quite ambitious. I was thinking seventy thirty since I've come up with the idea."

"Is that right? But you want me to travel and take all the risks? How fair is that?"

"Thirty is pretty good. That's a little over half a million dollars."

"I'd be happier with a million. Fifty-fifty or I'm out."

He sighed and looked at me. Part of me knew this was an easy negotiation. He had no other choice. "Fine. Fifty-fifty. Let's shake on it." We extended our arm and shook hands.

That night, I couldn't sleep even though I did my usual seven-mile walk. I kept tossing and turning, with nothing but worrisome thoughts occupying my head. Stocks plunging, diamonds missing, visiting Ursula... it all seemed surreal, like a bad dream. And then I was afraid to fall asleep because I feared the hyena would try to kill me again. My hunch was that my wife wouldn't let me go just yet. She haunted me in my dreams often, as if beckoning me to join her eternity. But I wasn't ready. Far from it. With that thought, I turned around once again and finally fell asleep.

The following day, I woke up at my usual time, bright and early. The kettle sound gave me an extra boost. My phone rang and startled me.

*Ring ring.*

I was going to let it ring until it stopped, but the sound seemed loud and annoying.

*Ring ring.*

I stood up and approached the phone.

"Hello?"

"Hey, Carl." Drew was on the other line. I recognized his voice immediately.

"Drew? What's up?"

"I'll meet you in front of Ursula's door in half an hour. Okay? Be presentable." I cared for my looks, and I was always presentable, even when I went for walks. It was Drew I was more concerned about. "Her apartment is 2G."

"Alright, Drew. I will see you in half an hour." With that, I hung up the phone and ran to the bathroom for a shave and a quick shower.

I was feeling apprehensive about Drew's and my plan. Maybe we had made a wrong decision after all. I felt like a sleazy man who was about to cheat out and take advantage of an old woman. But in her senile state of mind, she couldn't care less about the diamonds, I reasoned. Soon enough, I would meet and face Ursula—for the first time—myself. As I thought about the worst-case scenario, Drew's offer to take the lead during our visit felt like a tremendous relief.

When I arrived at Ursula's front door, Drew was already there. He wore tight slacks and a button-down shirt with a vest over it. His cologne, the sweet scent of honey, wafted through the air. He looked different, but it wasn't his clothes or the cologne that made it so. Did he also comb his hair? Brush his teeth? He had a huge smile and greeted me with a soft voice I hadn't heard coming out of him before. I didn't know what was happening with Drew, but I liked the new him, even if it was short-lived.

"Are you ready?" He asked.

"As ready as I can be."

"Good, good." I felt more at ease with Drew's obvious enthusiasm. How bad could this go in reality? The worst that could happen was the old woman would slam the door in our faces; maybe call the police on us. But I wasn't losing hope.

Drew knocked on her door, followed by dead silence. There were no sounds or commotion on the other side of the door. Maybe Ursula was still sleeping. Drew knocked again. Within seconds, we heard the old woman's voice. "Who is it?"

She sounded old and raspy, as if she were a chain smoker for decades.

"Hi, neighbor. It's Drew."

"Who?"

"Remember me, your gorgeous neighbor Drew?" He formed a huge smile on his face. I scoffed. Gorgeous? That was a bit of a stretch.

"What the hell do you want?"

"I'm here to say hello."

"What?"

Drew raised his voice by a few decibels. "I am here to say hello."

Silence. A few seconds later, the door opened up. There appeared the most fragile human being I had seen in a while. Her deep and coarse voice did not match her brittle looks. Her face was all wrinkly, and her body had diminished to a tiny size. Her hair was silver gray, soft looking, but messy from rubbing against a pillow. There was no smile on her, and I could tell she had had a hell of a life. And now dementia. I wanted to hug her at once and carry her in my arms and tell her I'd be there whenever, whatever she needed.

"What do you want?" Her voice brought me back to reality. Maybe she was stronger than I thought? She looked at us with her inquisitive eyes and waited for Drew to explain himself.

"Hi, there." He gave her a small wave like an innocent, sweet boy. "This is our neighbor, Carl. He lives on the third floor, and he wants to meet you."

"Yeah? Why?" She gave me a stern look, and I put

my head down out of embarrassment. This didn't seem to go well as I thought.

"He's an avid reader, and he thought you'd want to get together and share your stories." She looked at Drew, then me, then Drew, then me, and finally said. "Come on in."

His magic worked what appeared to be pure luck.

Her place was not what I expected to see. I thought I'd see old furniture to match her age, but her entire apartment was tastefully decorated with beautiful paintings hung on the wall, a leather couch in front of the windows decorated by elegant white drapes; a rocking chair was placed next to the couch; the carpet underneath was thick, made of wool with the patterns pleasing to the eye. On her kitchen table stood a vase overflowing with two dozen roses of various colors. This place didn't resemble one of a person with dementia. But what the hell did I know?

We sat down on the couch even though Ursula didn't extend an invitation. She sat on the rocking chair with some difficulty. When she leaned back, her feet were dangling in the air. She wobbled around until she made herself comfortable and then she gave us a long stare, expecting us to deliver a story she'd be delighted to hear.

"I told Carl you were originally from Germany." As he spoke, he nodded wildly.

"Ya," Ursula fired back.

"Tell us what was like growing up in Germany."

"What the hell do you care?" I looked at the carpet patterns below and counted the number of colors in each. Red, brown, some blue. I wanted to run away from the situation that was growing awkward. Oh, there's some yellow, too.

I raised my eyes from the carpet and looked at Ursula. Her eyes looked sad and lonely. I intervened.

"Speaking of Germany, I read in the newspaper yesterday that a Nazi officer hid diamonds in a secret place at the end of the war, and they're still missing." She raised her eyebrows.

"And?"

"I thought it was interesting they're still missing. After so many decades. Don't you?" I turned to Drew and his eyes rested on Ursula with his eyes wide open, as if he was waiting for her to spill out all her secrets. The room filled with silence, and Ursula kept her eyes on me like the hyena in my dreams.

"I suppose."

"Drew and I here. We were playing detectives for fun and tried to guess where the diamonds could be located." I smiled, hoping she'd join our game. "Listen to this. We speculated that there was a secret underground location where he hid them." At the corner of my eye, I felt Drew still nodding, his head moving wildly. "But we're still guessing where that secret place might be."

Silence ensued again, and I could tell Ursula was thinking.

"Go on," she said.

"Well, we thought the most likely town the diamonds could be hidden is Munich." I shrugged my shoulders. "But I don't know. Just a wild guess."

"O'ahu."

"Oh, wow, who?" Drew retorted. I looked at him and his face expression looked puzzled. Idiot.

"O'ahu," she repeated.

"You think diamonds could be in O'ahu?" I said.

"Ya." Ursula confirmed.

"That's an interesting thought." I looked at Drew and he still looked puzzled. As a mailman, I'd think his U.S. geography would be much better. Ursula stared at us, driving us to complete silence and awkwardness. We heard geese squeaking loudly outside; they must have felt the cold coming.

"Why would you think they are in O'ahu, Ursula?" I asked.

She paused to think, then finally shrugged, as if showing her signs of dementia. Her eyes were blank, and she pursed her lips. "Where else would they be if not in O'ahu?"

She sounded pretty confident, even though she didn't offer a sound explanation. I nodded in acknowledgment and appreciation of her trying to recall the events that took place so many decades ago. I would imagine it would be difficult to do so even with the healthiest of brains.

"Now, if you will excuse me, I need to take my nap." Ursula fidgeted in her chair and shot us a stern look.

"Anyway, it was really nice to meet you," I said. "We want you to know that we're here for you whenever you need something. I'm just a couple of steps away." She slightly nodded her head in gratitude. We were getting somewhere.

Both Drew and I stood up from the couch together like synchronized divers. I still wanted to hug Ursula, but she looked unapproachable and cold as she crossed her arms on her flat bosom. I turned around once again to bid her farewell and repeated that she should let us know if she ever needed anything from us. She nodded slightly again and offered a smile. I smiled back.

We exited her apartment, and Drew's first word flew out of his mouth: "Phew."

We walked side by side, me still trying to make out of all that just happened. Ursula was an old woman, with the signs of dementia, but she just gave us the biggest lead and clue to the diamonds' location. Things suddenly looked promising and hopeful.

"Let's go to my place and regroup," Drew said.

As soon as we entered his apartment, he took a cigarette out of his pack and lit it. He shaped his mouth like an O and exhaled small smoke rings that dissipated into the air.

"How come you didn't try to smoke at her place, but you did in mine yesterday?" I asked.

"You're different. You're my... partner." I shook my head at that. We were barely partners just yet. I was still skeptical about this entire plan. Of the whole wide world, what were the odds we would locate the diamonds? Would Ursula really dig deep into her memory and recall something that happened in 1945? And even if she did, would she trust us and share it with us?

"Whatever." I didn't have the energy to argue. "Let's get down to business."

"Sure."

"So Ursula gave us a clue that the diamonds could be in O'ahu. And by the way, O'ahu is in Hawaii, in case you didn't know."

"Sure."

"I don't think we got enough information out of her. We need to go back and keep digging. Don't you think?"

Drew combed his hair with his right pinky out

while holding the cigarette in his hand. "Agreed. Let's go back tomorrow and bring her blueberry muffins."

"Why blueberry muffins?"

"Everybody loves blueberry muffins. Besides, old ladies like to get gifts from young lads." He winked at me and smiled. I cringed.

"I'll see you tomorrow, Drew." With that, I exited the door and heard Drew scream YES behind me.

**3**

———

In the bright and early morning that followed the day I finally met Ursula, I approached my front door and noticed a white envelope slipped through the bottom crack. I quickly grabbed it and noticed a small piece of paper inside. I unfolded it and read:

21.2620° N, 157.8060° W

The writing was wobbly and written in blue ink. These numbers and letters were obviously geographic coordinates, which I was yet to discover to what location they belonged. Still sleepy and in my pajamas, I walked down the hall to Drew's place and knocked on his door. He opened it a few seconds later, with his head was peeking through the crack.

"Yes?"

I was holding the piece of the paper high in the air, "You gotta see this."

"Come in." He opened the door, revealing the scene I had regretted witnessing: he was wearing white underwear covered in yellow and brown spots in the back. I crinkled up my nose. All the unflattering things I was learning about my neighbor.

"You've got a map?"

"A map?" He ran to the other room and came back holding a map in his hand. We spread a world map on his couch and immediately a bunch of little dunes formed from the stuff piled up beneath. I said:

"My god, so hard to read anything. Do you have a globe?"

"A globe?" He grabbed keys from a pocket of the pants siting on the couch. Attached to them was a small globe keychain. "This?"

"Are you serious? You can barely see Brazil on that shit."

"Hold on." He walked back to the other room and came back with a much larger world map that he spread on the floor. "Will this do it?"

"Better." We knelt down on the floor, frantically trying to locate the coordinates. We went up and down the grid, at first disoriented, landing in China, then Canada, then—what was this tiny island?—Fiji until we landed on the spot. Hawaii.

"Look at this, will you!" I exclaimed. "Ursula said yesterday that the diamonds could be in O'ahu. And here it is, the coordinates to our treasure." I smiled ear to ear.

Drew lifted his arms overhead and widened his eyes. As big as a house. "Holy moly. We're rich!"

"Hold on to your horses, man. We're not rich just yet. Not until I have those diamonds in my hands."

"Fair enough."

"I'll be calling a travel agency today to book a plane ticket to Hawaii." I already had a plan in my head, which sounded perfect: as soon as I got to Hawaii, I would embark on searching for the location based on the coordinates Ursula gave us. Once I got a hold of the diamonds, I'd return home and live happily ever after. Okay, maybe I'd visit a beach or two while I was already there.

"Carl." Drew's eyes watered up with tears. "I can't believe this is happening."

I exited his apartment and instead of going back home; I stopped by the lobby to get my daily newspaper. I rushed to my apartment to get ready for my usual daily walk.

On my way out, it surprised me to see Drew in the foyer, sorting out the mail.

"Hey, Drew. What are you doing sorting out mail so early?"

He lifted his head to look at me and said, "I always sort the mail around this time. I don't know what you're talking about."

I smiled at him and thought I was probably going nuts and forgetting his usual mail delivery time.

"I was about to go for a walk."

"Okay." Drew sounded puzzled. He put his head down and went on with his business.

"I'm really excited about going to Hawaii."

Drew lifted his head, looked at me, dropped his head down, and said nothing. He returned to his sorting task.

"I'm also excited to know that we have clues."

Drew looked at me again and snared, "Hey, listen, I'm busy here and need to concentrate. Mind talking to someone else?"

I looked around and saw no one but Drew in my proximity.

"Sure. Sorry, Drew." Drew shook his head as I waved at him, exiting from his sight.

When I returned from my walk, I pulled a phone book out of a drawer of the hallway dresser and found the phone number for a local travel agency. The phone rang and a youngish sounding lady answered on the other side:

"Bold World Travel Agency, how may I help you?"

"Yes, my name is Carl Walker, and I'd like to buy a plane ticket to Hawaii, please."

"Yes, sir. Smoking or non-smoking section."

"Non-smoking." I wished they'd ban smoking on the planes already.

She took down all of my other information and asked me whether I wanted to pick up my ticket or have it mailed. I would, of course, pick it up. A reason to go on a walk.

When the young lady called me to let me know my plane ticket was ready, the day turned gloomy and rainy. I stood by my living room window and watched the raindrops slide down the glass. The rain was falling down with a vengeance as if a god was mourning a sad loss. One thing I did hate was rain, but my legs urged me to step outside despite the calamity.

The travel agency wasn't located too far from my apartment. It stood in a corner of an old building, the sign on the awning old and washed out. I shook and closed my umbrella before I entered. At the counter stood a beautiful young woman smiling at me, as if she had been waiting for my arrival all along and was happy to see me. We exchanged the niceties before I told her I was there to pick up my plane ticket.

"Of course, Mr. Walker." She opened up a drawer and pulled an envelope from it. "Here you are."

She pushed the envelope through the small window in the plexiglass between us. "Can I offer you anything else while you're here? Perhaps surfing lessons? It's part of a lodging package you can purchase through our agency."

When I was younger, I'd go to the YMCA and swim dozens of laps in early mornings, but surfing, I imagined, would never be my cup of tea.

"That is kind of you, but I'll pass." She still smiled and bid me a safe trip and farewell.

"Till later, Mr. Walker."

The rain had dwindled, and I kept my umbrella shut. As the raindrops hit my face, I clenched my left fist and felt a sense of angst wash over me. What did I get myself into? If it wasn't for stocks' value plummeting, I wouldn't even consider this crazy adventure. But now that I paved my path to hunting for the diamonds in certainty, with a plane ticket in my pocket, there was no point of return. The following day, I was on my way to the lush island thousands of miles away from home.

And there my journey began.

* * *

A yellow taxi pulled over in front of my building at six a.m. I dragged my suitcase on the ground, making noise, wondering if it awoke anyone in the building. Did Ursula have light sleep? Or did she sleep like a log? I had not stopped by Drew's place to bid him farewell. He said he would have loved to join me, but his request for time off from work would be difficult to approve and thus, I was all alone on this journey. But I told him I'd call him from Hawaii and give him frequent updates. He said he'd hang by the phone and make sure he was available when I called.

"Don't forget the six-hour difference," I forewarned him. His eyes looked up and his lips moved like he was counting.

"Okay. I'll stand by, Carl."

In the taxi car, a young man of dark skin was at the wheel; he turned around and greeted me with a smile, his large teeth as white as snow.

"Hi, sir." I sensed an African accent. "Logan airport?"

"Correct." I sat down in the back seat and off we headed to the Boston International airport.

The plane ride was going to be long, with a stopover in San Francisco. Over ten hours. How I was going to manage not to walk for that long worried me already. I pictured myself pacing up and down between the aisles endlessly. That seemed my only option. But the ultimate reward of arriving on the island and getting a hold of the treasure was indescribable. It would be all worth it in the end.

As suspected, the flights to Hawaii were uneventful. When I arrived, I was happy to feel the warm breeze from the Pacific Ocean and the humid tropical air. Boston was wrapping itself up in colder days; winter wasn't my favorite season. The Boston blizzard of 1978 still lingered in my mind like a buzzing mosquito ready to bite. Every winter, I couldn't help but remember when I was stuck in my office, my car parked in the front, unable to move, buried in a cold white heap. That evening, after work, I ended up walking through three feet of snow to my house. Walk was tedious and slow, but it was my only form of transport. It took me four hours to get home that night, my hands and feet nearly freezing. When I entered the house, I nearly cried from the anger that had accumulated inside me.

The Hawaii air was a pleasant touch. I hailed a cab in front of the airport, and it pulled over immediately.

"Where to?" The taxi driver yelled out of the car.

"Moana Surfrider."

"Get in." I sat in the back and I could see the driver's eyes resting on me through the back-view mirror. "Business or leisure?"

"What?" I was too tired and jet lagged to exchange words.

He raised his voice and asked again, "Business or leisure?"

I paused, trying to think of the best answer so he wouldn't engage again. "Leisure."

"Ah, you're in the right place, then. A lot to do here. If you like to water surf, I recommend the North Shore. Waves there are crazy."

Then I remembered I had to find the geographic coordinates that Ursula gave us. Without proper tools, it could take me forever.

"Hey, you know this island well, right?"

"It's a small island."

I pulled the piece of paper with the coordinates and placed it in his direction. "Any idea how to find this location?"

I saw him checking out the piece of paper via the mirror. "What is that?"

"Geographic coordinates." I tried to find an easy way to get to my location and was too eager to begin my search.

"I'm a cab driver, but I'm no scientist. Unless someone comes up with a device to get me from one place to another, I'm on my own. If I don't know the location of a place, I need to rely on a map with actual names."

"Fine." I put the paper back in my pocket.

When we arrived at the hotel, I paid the driver and swiftly exited the car. As I set foot on the land, the beauty of my surroundings took my breath away. On one side of the hotel was a major street, and across the street were stores of all kinds. In the street's corner was a grocery store, which I was sure would come in handy during my stay. On the other side of the hotel was the beach and the ocean beyond, sitting on a vast horizon. The ocean was unusually calm that night. The crescent moon gave some light to the land. As I stood facing the hotel, I saw a hill on my left side standing up like a single tooth in a baby's mouth. Awkward and odd. As I looked at the untouched nature, I almost forgot why I was there. This would be a quick trip, after all. But the biggest challenge of locating the diamonds remained.

I settled in my hotel room, a tiny space with a single bed and a dresser on the opposite side. The view of the ocean was fabulous. I rested my eyes on the sky and, as I focused more, the number of flickering stars was increasing.

I felt tired. I went to bed and fell asleep almost immediately.

I woke up somber and still tired. The sun was above the ocean already; I looked at my watch, but it was only six am. I heard a rooster crowing nearby. A rooster. What was a rooster doing under my balcony? I put on my shorts and a T-shirt and walked up to the reception area. My eyes were half-closed. Through my narrow eye openings, I saw a man and a woman standing behind the reception counter. The woman lifted her head and when she saw me, she greeted me with a huge smile: "Aloha, sir. How can we help you?"

"Rooster." I was pointing with my finger outside. The woman laughed.

"Ah yes, the roosters."

"They woke me up. What's with the roosters? Why do you have them at the hotel?"

The woman let a laugh out again. "They don't belong to the hotel, sir. They're wild."

"Wild roosters. How on earth did that happen?"

"Blame it on Hurricane Iwa. 1982."

"What does the hurricane have to do with roosters?" I was tired, but my curious mind was in full gear.

"When the hurricane came, they escaped the cops and mixed with feral chickens. So, there."

"Do they crow every morning?"

"Every single morning, sir." She opened a drawer of her reception desk and pulled out a small bag. "If you need earplugs, please take these." She extended her arm with the bag in her hand, her serious eyes meeting mine and signaling there was no other compromise.

I reached for the bag and thanked her. Back in my room, I spread my arms and legs on the bed and looked up at the ceiling. How many more surprises would Hawaii show me? I opened up the small bag the receptionist gave me and put the earplugs in my ears. My eyes felt heavy, and they involuntarily closed, putting me to sleep. There was a long day ahead of me. I needed my rest.

The earplugs worked. When I woke up, it was almost noon. A different time zone messed up my biological clock. Fully rested, I now panicked about starting my day late and not being able to accomplish my only mission. I brushed my teeth and washed my face and found the most comfortable clothes I had. My sneakers were my rescue from a long day.

At the lobby, I approached the same woman I spoke to this morning, but she didn't seem to recognize me right away. I cleaned up a bit and my hair wasn't as messy, so I could see why she had me confused with the earlier version of Carl. When I greeted her with 'hello again,' she widened her eyes and put her hand on her mouth, out of embarrassment.

"Sir, I didn't recognize you at first. I apologize. Mr. Walker? Can I help you?"

I got the piece of paper out of my pocket and said, "I need to get to a certain location, and I have the coordinates for it. Now, I need help to get to it, so I'm asking if you'd have any clue how."

I showed her the coordinates, and she understood immediately. I was glad I didn't need to explain what they were.

"Ah, yes, Mr. Walker. People often come to us asking about this location. It's quite popular here." She smiled.

"It is?" A small dose of defeat came over me and I felt like my mission might have been somehow bombed. "What is this place? What's so special about it?"

"Why it's Diamond Head, Mr. Walker! Anyone who comes to visit O'ahu must climb Diamond Head."

"But what is it?"

"It's a hill formed by an ancient volcano. There's a path that takes you to the very top and you can then see the ocean stretching for miles on one side and Waikiki on the other side. The views are quite spectacular."

"A hill?" I leaned forward and widened my eyes. What would diamonds do on a hill? And what coincidence was it that the hill was named Diamond Head? Was it named after our treasure? Things were getting more confusing. Did Ursula, in her demented mind, give me the wrong coordinates?

"Yes, Mr. Walker. I suggest you visit during the week, since weekends can be overcrowded with tourists." She leaned down to grab something, then propped herself back up. "We don't offer this to everyone, but you can borrow this on your trip."

She handed me a device I had never seen before. It was the size of a human palm, bulky, and had a small screen in the front and buttons on the side.

"I appreciate your generosity. But what is it?"

"It's a location tracking device. It tells you where you are in any given place."

"Whoa!" I couldn't believe my eyes and ears. "Whoa! You just made my day…"

"Emily."

"Emily. Thanks, Emily."

"You're welcome. It's only a couple of miles down the road from here."

I took the device and headed out for the door. Diamond Head, according to Emily's description, wasn't too far.

## 4

The clouds in the sky disappeared completely by 2 p.m., leaving the sun all on its lonesome. It was getting hot. The distance between the hotel and Diamond Head was a mere 2.7 miles. I could get there in no time, even by foot, but I still needed to find the exact location for the diamonds. The tracking device would help make that happen.

I arrived at the Diamond Head base to an empty parking lot except for a couple of cars. On my left side was an extensive field that was slowly turning into a hill in a distance. On my right were public bathrooms, a water fountain in the front. Ahead of me was a paved path that led to the hilltop. I quickened my steps, knowing each one got me closer to the diamonds. The device in my hand was getting soaked from my palms sweat. I was trying to be careful not to drop it. Breaking it would lead to a colossal failure. The path was paved in concrete, but as I advanced toward the top, it was getting steeper and narrower, with fewer trees and plants around.

The views were becoming more vast and the Pacific Ocean wider as I walked. A woman with a young child was walking in the opposite direction and talking in German. I nodded as they came closer.

"Hello," the woman said to me in a heavy accent as she nearly brushed against my shoulder. She stopped and waited for me to reciprocate. Her upper front teeth were separated, and she had freckles all over the face. A bucket hat covered her sunshiny blonde hair. "May I ask you something, please?"

"Yeah, sure."

"My son wants to see the bunker from World War II, but I don't know where it's located." The child grabbed her hand and looked at me with a devious smile. "Do you know?"

"The bunker?" I repeated. "I didn't even know there was a bunker on the island."

"Indeed." She smiled. "Apparently, it's on a big ranch somewhere on the island, but I cannot figure out what ranch. There are so many."

"Well, I'm sorry. I'm of no help. But I hope you and your son will find it soon and visit." The boy looked disappointed, and his eyes drooped down. "You have a nice rest of the day, ma'am."

We parted ways, and I continued walking up the hill. A few minutes later, I arrived at an observation deck where nearly the 360 view was breathtaking. Was I dreaming? I almost felt like I was about to gain a pair of wings and flop them around until I flew above and coasted over the ocean. I wanted to fly so badly and have the bird's-eye of this beautiful piece of land. I grabbed the railing in front of me, and I sighed deeply as I stared into the oblivion.

The breeze was caressing my face, and the slight wind was making a buzzing sound in my ears. If heaven existed, it would resemble this view. On the other side of the deck, I could see Waikiki sitting along the ocean; tall buildings stretching up to the sky looking like LEGO blocks from the distance. I couldn't see anything else—no people, no cars, nothing—and I felt I was in an apocalypse movie left alone to fend for myself on the planet.

That was ideal. I didn't want anyone to be around when I searched for the diamonds. I continued going up the hill, and the path was getting even steeper and narrower. It was at a time like this I was grateful for having the proclivity to walk all the time. Being in shape was needed for a path like this one.

I came to a narrow tunnel made of pure rock. A

couple of people coming from the opposite direction were talking, with the sound of their voices amplified. We crossed each other's path, making room for each other to pass. Now I was all alone. When I came to the end of the tunnel, I brought the device closer to my face to examine what it could do. I pushed the ON button, and suddenly numbers and letters appeared on the screen, what clearly seemed to be geographic coordinates. I compared them to the one I had on the piece of paper and realized the diamond location was only feet away.

My nerves rattled, so I sat down to compose myself. I brushed my hair with my arm to clean the sweat off. The blue sky was the only thing I saw. I looked at the device again, and I stood up to get closer to the coordinates where the diamonds were located. My steps were slow and measured and I finally found myself on the location.

Confused and baffled by the sight in front of me, I gasped, "What?"

What stood before me was a large rock, as big as a small house. I started walking around it in circles, checking out the device like a maniac. Maybe Ursula missed a digit or two? The numbers were changing to show the new coordinates as I moved, and they were nothing like what I had on the piece of paper. Could there be margin of error? Was it possible that the diamonds could be within feet of the location?

I looked around, and there were rocks upon rocks. There was no way the diamonds were hidden in the rocks unless there were cracks somewhere. I carefully examined for any holes, but there were none.

I couldn't help but think of The Rime of the Ancient Mariner poem: water, water everywhere, nor any drop to drink. Rocks, rocks everywhere, nor any diamonds in sight.

I lied down on a rock—it was flat and hot; I was exasperated. Things did not go as planned, and now I wondered if Ursula was messing with us all along. It was entirely naïve of us to trust a lady with dementia. As I felt the sun shining on me as I lay down, I devised a new plan.

But then, out of nowhere, my encounter with the German woman flashed in front of me. The information she gave me left a peculiar thought in my subconscious. A bunker from World War II. Could it be possible that the diamonds were left in the bunker as opposed to Diamond Head? Come to think of it, leaving them anywhere on a hill made little sense. How would the diamonds get there?

A more likely scenario was that the diamonds got transported to a place that was remote and safe.

I rushed down the path, holding onto the device like it was a life-saving object. In less than ten minutes, I was at the base, looking for a payphone.

Since there weren't any there, I advanced to the suburban area below the hill and found myself on a somewhat bustling main street with cars rushing to places and honking at each other. I walked and walked until a payphone appeared in front of me.

I frantically searched for coins inside my pocket and unearthed a few quarters. The quarters dinged as I placed them in the slot. Dialing Drew—seven, eight, one, five, five, five, zero, nine, three, two.

*Ring ring.*

It was 3 p.m., 9 p.m. in Boston.

*Ring ring.*

"Pick up the phone!" I was screaming. A passerby heard me as he walked by and made an arch around me to avoid my outburst.

*Ring ring.*

"Son of a bitch!" I hung up the phone, and the quarters spit out at the bottom of the phone. I grabbed them and walked away.

Drew wasn't home. Maybe for the best. I had better break the news to him in the comfort of my room, where no one could eavesdrop on my conversation. Somewhere near Diamond Head was a beach I visited for a brief rest. The day had turned out exhausting and unpredictable.

When I arrived at the beach, I took off my sneakers to feel the sand specks under my feet. The sand was warm and inviting. The beach was nearly empty, with only a couple of women sitting in their chairs in a far distance. Their faces were covered with their hats. The birds were flying overhead and calling each other as they cut through the air. The ocean was wavy, but the waves weren't large enough to call for surfing. With only the ocean's sound traveling to my ears, I felt calm at last.

I lay close to the water and closed my eyes. I replayed all the things that had happened since Drew broke the news about the secret place with diamonds and I was realizing I became desperate to locate them as my future suddenly became uncertain. With the stock market crashing, I ran to my bank to check the balance on my account and—lo-and-behold—I had lost hundreds of thousands of dollars. My retirement was in ruins. The immediate feeling of unease and uncertainty came over me. I could not picture myself worrying about my finances, or worse yet, about changing my lifestyle. I couldn't go back to the corporate world and sit at a desk day-in, day-out. Those days were over for me. Forever. I'd rather look for diamonds and I'd take my time to do so. I knew it would be worthwhile. My future would no longer be in question. I'd be the king of my invisible palace, the ruler of my wonderful world.

As my resolve to find the diamonds was confirmed, my mind quieted down. I was lying on the beach—I didn't know for how long—when suddenly, swooooosh! The ocean grabbed me with its arms and I became helpless in its embrace. An enormous wave carried me toward the depths of the ocean. I tried to get out of its claws, but the wave was powerful and vicious. I swirled around in the wave, unable to control any of my movements. For a split second, I got to the water's surface, caught a breath or two, but then another wave dragged me under, and it carried me at the speed of light. I opened my eyes, and in the corner, I thought I had seen a human on a surfing board passing me by. My right arm lifted as if calling someone for help, but the wave violently stole me from underneath and I traveled through the water like a fish caught on a line.

Everything was happening so fast that I couldn't think of a way to get back to the shore. In a near distance, I saw a large fin of what could belong to a shark, and I panicked. It was going to attack me. In an instant, I thought of the movie "Jaws" and I feared I might end up legless or armless. At that moment, nothing mattered. I didn't care about the diamonds, I just wanted to escape from the shark. But the fin moved away, and all that was left around me was the wild water. I got the hang of its power and grit, and I slowly regained strength. I let my body relax, so I could move along with the waves; it was when I fought it that nature fought back more fiercely.

Positioned on my back, the waves carried me back to the shore. When I opened my eyes and saw the beach on the horizon, I realized it was safe again.

I came up to the shore and lay on the beach, and the device was sitting next to me untouched. The sun was creeping down the horizon. The crescent moon was showing its face in all its glory. It wasn't dark just yet, though; the day was bidding its farewell. My body seemed untouched. There were no dents or bruises or cuts. Only luck could be attributed to being in one piece after the turbulent time in the ocean. I stood up from the sand, put on my sneakers, took the device in my head, and headed to the hotel.

When I arrived, Emily was no longer at the reception. Her shift must have been over, and a young man replaced her. I approached the reception and greeted him.

"Hello. I need to know if anyone called me while I was out."

"What's your room number, sir?"

"212."

He checked something behind the counter and announced, "No, sir. No calls."

Disappointed, I walked away without saying a word.

My room seemed dark, so I flipped the light switch. I came up to the phone and dialed Drew.

*Ring ring.*

"Hello?"

"Where the hell have you been?" I screamed into the phone receiver.

"I'm here. Did you call earlier?"

"Yes, I called you earlier. I'm here risking my life, and you're nowhere to be found."

"Risking your life? Why, what happened?"

"I was swallowed into the ocean today. I almost died. The waves were enormous. I was helpless, Drew. I could have died."

"How did you end up in the ocean, Carl? Don't you know how to swim?"

"Yes, of course I know how to swim! I was the best swimmer at YCMA back in the day. And does it matter how I ended up in the water?"

"I guess it doesn't. I'm glad to hear you're okay."

Silence. I still needed time to trust Drew fully. He was my true partner in this hunt, and I needed to be reassured. I was about to break the news about my today's discovery, and I didn't know how he'd react.

"Well, I called you earlier today to let you know I found the location."

"And?" I sensed excitement in his voice. I'd imagine he was hoping for the good news. That the mission was easy and swift. If that was his expectation, he wouldn't be happy with what I was about to say next.

I lowered my voice, so nobody could hear me from the outside of the walls of my room: "There's nothing. Absolutely nothing there."

"What do you mean, nothing?"

"If rocks count as something, then yeah. Otherwise, nothing. We've been fooled, Drew. Fooled." Silence ensued again.

"Are you sure?"

"Yes, I am sure!"

"Sounds like I need to visit Ursula again and dig for more information out of her. Agree?"

"Ask her about a bunker. Apparently, there's a bunker from World War II on the island, and I suspect the diamonds could be there."

"Sure, Carl. I'll ask her about the bunker. Hopefully, we will get to the bottom of it. No pun intended." He laughed. Idiot.

"I'll call tomorrow at the same time and find out what you've come up with. Bring her blueberry muffins."

"Good idea." With that, we both hung up the phone. My stomach growled, telling me it was time to eat. The hotel had a restaurant on the beach, and I ate dinner there.

I took a quick shower and slipped into my white button-down shirt and black slacks. It was a rare occasion for me to dress up. The cologne smell wafted through the air and filled the hallway as soon I stepped outside of my room. As I was locking the door, at the corner of my eye, I noticed a swift movement at the very end of the hallway. I thought I had seen someone quickly disappear from behind the wall, and that someone, I felt with my gut, was here to follow me. I leaned backward to see if the person would make its appearance again, but the hallway looked as empty and dark as a coffin.

The person was watching me as I took the key out of the lock. I quickened the pace in case I could still catch sight of him (or her), but there was nobody. I could hear the TV sound behind the walls in one room, and people talking in the other one. On my way to the restaurant, I wondered who could follow me. Whoever that person was must have known what I was after and why I was here. But how did they find out? Did Drew send someone to the island, to wait for me to get ahold of the diamonds, and then have this person kill me? I had to be smart about all this. I'd wait and see what he had to tell me tomorrow once he spoke with Ursula.

**5**

———

The restaurant looked open and airy as several tables sat on the stony deck shaped like a squared U. The waiter greeted me pleasantly and walked me to my table. He moved a chair and invited me to sit down.

"Please, sir." I followed his instructions and sat down on the chair. A busboy came up to my table and poured a glass of water while smiling at me. He disappeared into a corner, and I took the menu to see what my dinner options were, but my hungry stomach could opt in for just about anything. I decided on salmon. As I looked around to see if anyone might watch or follow me, I caught a sight of her: one of the most beautiful women I had ever seen.

As she entered the restaurant, her hips moved

like gentle waves; her hair was dark, long and silky. Her skin was tan like gold. She had full lips and was wearing red lipstick. Her eyelashes were dancing as she blinked and smiled. She brought in a certain aura, like a daydream that I didn't want to end. Her presence was undeniable. I resolved immediately I had to meet her, somehow. Encountering this goddess, I felt even my wife would forgive me.

My food arrived shortly after, and as I ate my meal, I kept my eyes on the woman. She was sitting at the bar in the middle of the restaurant and gesturing something to the bartender. He said something that made her laugh out loud. Her laughter sounded like a symphony.

The waiter came and offered a dessert menu. I shook my head and told him I was ready for the check. When I paid my bill, I boldly walked up to the bar and stood next to the woman, waiting for the bartender to come up. She was on my left side, and I felt her body emanate warmth and magnetism. I turned toward her, and our eyes met. Her smile relaxed me and made me feel I was reunited with a long-lost friend after many years.

"Hi," I said.

"Hello." Her smile lingered.

"Beautiful evening, is it not?" I didn't know what else to say. Didn't everyone talk about the weather when they first met?

"Indeed."

The bartender came up to me and asked what I wanted to order. I wasn't much of a drinker; in fact, I didn't drink alcohol at all, but I'd look a fool if I had ordered a glass of water. I turned back to the woman and asked, "Can I buy you a drink?" She gave me a flirtatious smile and a slight nod.

"If you insist."

"Whatever the lady wants. And I'll have a glass of scotch on rocks."

The bartender took our order and walked away.

"What's the handsome gentleman doing buying drinks to unknown women?"

"You looked like you needed company. And I needed company. So, why not?" she laughed at that.

"What brings you here?"

"I was hungry, and I needed to eat. My room is right there." I pointed at the dark room with a balcony on the second floor. She laughed again.

"Yeah, alright. I meant what brings you to Hawaii? You don't look like a local for sure."

"Ah yes. Hawaii." I got myself in a pickle. If I told her the truth, she could tell someone, and our secret about the diamond hunt would be revealed. But if I didn't tell her, I'd feel terrible about lying. So, what did I do? I told her, "I'm here for leisure. How about you?"

Her eyes looked at me with depth and curiosity.

Her long eyelashes waved at me as if she herself had a secret.

"I'm here for a conference. My boss sent me to learn a thing or two about marketing."

"And? Are you learning anything?"

"So far, so good." She laughed. "But I'd rather lay on the beach and get some suntan."

"Speaking of the beach," I wanted to entertain her a little, "I almost died today."

"What? Died?" Her eyes widened. "What happened?"

"Well, I was lying on the beach when suddenly, a wave pulled me in. The waves kept taking me into the depths and I couldn't control my body movements at all. And I'm pretty sure that I saw a shark nearby, but it left me alone."

"This really happened to you?" She sounded unamused.

"Yeah, sure did."

"What time did it happen??

"Oh, I don't know. Maybe between four and five."

"Four and five? I took a walk along the beach around that time, and the ocean was as smooth as glass."

"Impossible!"

"I have photos to prove it. I can show them to you as soon as I have the film developed."

"How will I know you took them today?"

"I guess you won't. You'll just need to trust me." She smiled. The bartender came and put our drinks on the bar. We grabbed our glasses and brought them together.

"Cheers!" we said at the same time and took a sip from our glass. While her hand was up in the air, I took a peek at her finger and saw no ring. She was single. I couldn't believe it. The scotch tasted like someone put fire in my mouth. The flavor went from sweet to bitter to ash-like taste in a matter of seconds. She looked at me and laughed. I closed my eyes to compose myself.

"You don't seem well." I opened my eyes, and the amused look on her face made everything better.

"I'm fine." I gazed toward the main hotel door and noticed a man wearing all black standing in the middle of the lobby and staring at me. His hands were in his pockets, and he had a conspicuous smile. Our eyes met, and he then turned around quickly and walked out of the hotel. "Excuse me, I'll be right back."

I rushed in his direction, hoping to catch him in his act. Who was he? Why was he following me? I needed to find out as soon as possible.

I went outside and thought I had seen the man cross the street to the other side and disappear from a building corner. I stood on the curb and waited for a couple of cars to go by before I could cross the street. The stoplight was green, but I jaywalked like I owned the city. I ran behind the corner of the building and the black figure was walking far in the distance. He took a left turn, and I ran to not lose sight of him. I took the same left and expected he'd be nearby, but he was nowhere to be found. On my right side was a street parallel to the main street, where only a few cars passed by. Ahead of me was a long curbside that led to several intersections, and in between were tall buildings and trees competing for heights. But the man was nowhere to be found. I kept walking in hopes he'd somehow reappear, but all the probable places he could be in were void of people.

I tried to plant his appearance into my memory: he was about six feet tall; he had a ponytail and a moustache. His features were manly, and he moved swiftly.

But who was he? And why did he follow me? He was gone. He looked awfully familiar, like I had seen him many times before. His moves and his smile were ones I had seen before, I was certain. But where had I seen him? I racked my brain to remember, but no one came to mind. I must have been dreaming again, and my dreams probably melted with my reality.

It was killing me, though. I wanted to know, and I needed to get rid of the man. He seemed like trouble and an imposition to my well-designed plan. I could not let him ruin my plans, my life.

When I returned to the restaurant, it was still hopping with customers. At tables sat mostly couples; some happy looking and some staring in front, as if hoping they'd be somewhere else at that moment. I returned to the bar to rejoin the lady I met, but she was no longer there. I looked around, hoping she'd maybe took a walk to the beach, only a few feet distance, but I didn't find her. Maybe she went to the restroom.

A considerable amount of time passed, and she wasn't coming back. I looked at my watch and saw it was almost eight. The bartender came up to me and asked me if I wanted anything else.

"I have a question." I was only focused on the woman.

"Yes, sir?"

"What happened to the woman I was talking to earlier?"

"What woman?"

"The one with long black hair, red lipstick. I bought her a drink, remember?"

"I don't know what you're talking about, sir. I don't remember any black-haired woman."

"Seriously? She was just here with me."

"I see way too many people here. I can't remember everyone. Sir, if you will now excuse me.

The bar is getting busy." With that, he turned around and disappeared to the other side of the bar.

I looked around to find a trace of the goddess, but she was nowhere to be found. I didn't catch her name. If I had, I could have looked her up at the hotel reception. I only hoped that she was staying at the same hotel, or she'd cross my path again. Somewhat sad, my evening ended without one last look at the woman, I went back to my room and devised a plan on how to find her.

**6**

———

Cock-a-doodle-doo.
　　*Cock-a-doodle-doo.*
　　*Cock-a-doodle-doo.*
*Cock-a-doodle-doo.*
*Cock-a-doodle-doo.*

"Mother... shut the hell up!" The roosters outside were relentless. Even the earplugs couldn't help the vocal force they were producing outside. I looked at my watch and noticed it was four a.m. Too early to wake up and start the day.

My mind went to the woman I met. A thought of her woke me up and I couldn't help but reflect on my encounter with her. If I only had asked for her name. What was I thinking?

I crossed my arms behind my head and stared at the ceiling. A smile formed on my face as I thought of... Lillian. I gave her that name. She looked like a Lillian. Beautiful and bright as a lily. Was I falling in love? Or lust? What about my wife? Would she forgive me if I fell in love? She hadn't been in my dreams for a while. Maybe she was finally letting me move on to find someone new in life. She'd understand that I couldn't be a loner for the rest of my life. I was relatively still young, a lot of love to share. Everything could change in an instant if I could find her again. Lillian.

I'd find out where she lived and write her letters. She would write letters back to me. We'd keep connected, learn about each other, grow something special between us until the fate reunited us to be in each other's arms forever. I'd write often, open up my heart, and tell her everything that lingered in my mind.

*DEAR LILLIAN,*

*It is with a heavy heart that I'm writing this letter now. I wish we had acquainted ourselves the night we met in Hawaii. The second I saw you took my breath away and I swear to God, you are the most beautiful woman I've ever laid my eyes on. I regretted not asking you your name, or anything about you, but you understand that a man rarely knows what to ask of a woman when he is so taken by her. I welcomed meeting you and really enjoyed talking with you, albeit in a short amount of time. It made me sad that, upon returning to the bar, you were gone for the night, but the following morning, I asked the receptionist about you and they knew exactly who you were. I guess a woman like you is unforgettable, Lillian. They told me you checked out the following morning and went back home. It devastated me to hear the news. Although it's against their policy, I begged them to give your address. It took many hours of convincing, but they finally caved. So, you live in Maine? I'm glad to hear that you're not that far from me, Lillian. You can visit me anytime if your heart desires so. I would love to see you again. Until then, my letters will reach you as often as possible.*

*With love,*
*Carl Walker*

As I FORMULATED the letter in my head, the telephone startled me.

*Ring ring.*

I stood up and answered the phone at the second ring.

"Hello?"

"Hey, Carl, it's Drew."

"Drew. You know what time it is in Hawaii?"

"Yeah. Four thirty am, why?"

I rolled my eyes and shook my head. "Never mind. What's up, Drew?"

"I went to visit Ursula like we talked yesterday. No mention of the bunker."

"Did you ask her, or did she not say anything?"

"I said something about a bunker in Hawaii and she just stared at me."

"That's not good."

"No. I didn't think she thought the diamonds were there. She gave no clues to that at all."

"Listen, Drew. I think we have another problem at hand."

"What is it, Carl?"

"I think someone is following me."

"Really? Who could it be? Only you and I know about the diamonds."

"Is that right, Drew?"

"What do you mean? You think I'd tell someone our plan? I'm not that clever, Carl. You don't need to worry about me. Besides, are you sure they are following you?"

"Positively sure. TA guy with a moustache and a ponytail was watching me at dinner.The second I started walking in his direction, he ran away."

"Did he also have a goatee?"

"No. Why?"

"Just wondering. Most men have a goatee with a moustache."

"Freddie Mercury doesn't." I wanted to prove him wrong.

"I guess you're right. But the moustache alone looks good on him."

"Drew, how's all this relevant right now? Can we talk about what's next?"

"Come home?"

"Are you sure? You don't think there's more digging to do with Ursula?" I was desperate to keep trying. Plus, I'd buy myself some extra time and try to locate Lillian.

"I can certainly try, but this morning was a disaster. She just kept staring at me during my visit, and she only nodded when I handed her the muffins. She couldn't even say 'thank you'? It was very uncomfortable."

"Alright. I'm going to stay a couple of more days and go back to the site one more time. Maybe fresh eyes will have more luck. In the meantime, go see Ursula again and ask her explicitly about what she remembers about that day back in 1945. The more info you get out of her, the better."

"I can try, but no promises." He made a pause. "Is that... do I hear roosters in the background?"

"Don't even go there. I'll talk to you tomorrow, Drew. Goodbye." I hung up the phone and went back to my bed.

I tossed and turned, tossed and turned, and I

couldn't fall back to sleep. At six, I got up and head down to the lobby. I wore the same slacks and button-down shirt I wore last night, and a pair of sneakers. At the lobby, I grabbed the daily newspaper and headed to the restaurant for breakfast. I sat at the same table from last night and was soon greeted by a waiter. A minute later, he brought me coffee and bread with butter. I put down the newspaper on the table and, with my being tired-eyed, it remained untouched. I ate my breakfast and headed to speak to someone at the reception.

"Hello. Good morning."

"Aloha, Mr. Walker." Emily was back for her shift. She recognized me this time. "What can I do for you? Did you enjoy your walk yesterday?"

"Absolutely delighted. The island is beautiful. Gorgeous."

"Wonderful to hear. Did the device help?"

"Oh, more than you think. Thank you for lending it."

"Excellent. Well, I'll need it back when you're ready. We have other guests in the hotel who like to explore the island."

"Yes, of course. I will return it today." I found an excellent opportunity to segue into my question. "Speaking of other guests, would you know if a certain woman is staying at your hotel?"

"What's her name? I can look her up."

"That's the problem. I don't have her name. I only know what she looks like."

She smiled the sarcastic smile and said, "Mr. Walker, this is a big hotel. We don't track our guests by their looks."

"I understand. But this woman has quite distinct features."

"Mr. Walker…"

"Hear me out, please." I gave her the exact description of her, not skipping a beat, and Emily's face suddenly brightened up.

"Ah, yes, of course. That's our guest Lillian."

"Lillian? Did you say Lillian?"

"Indeed. She was here for a conference, but I'm sad to say she left for home early this morning."

"She… she left?"

"Yes. I checked her out around five this morning. She had an early connection flight home."

"Oh." My heart sank. "Would it be possible to get her home address? She left something with me and I must return it to her."

"I'm afraid no can do. It is against the hotel policy to give out the personal information of our guests."

"Emily." I looked at her with the puppy eyes. "Lillian absolutely must have the item she left with me. Or else her life could be in danger."

She stared at me with desperate eyes and remained silent. "Let me talk to my supervisor."

She turned around and disappeared behind the wall. A couple of minutes later, she returned with the same desperate look on her face, which probably meant she didn't get far.

"Mr. Walker, my supervisor was kind enough to agree for me to share the woman's full name, but I cannot give out her address. She can sue the hotel if I did."

Her name was good enough. "What is it?"

"It's Lillian Daisy."

"You're so very kind, Emily. I don't know how to thank you." She looked at me coldly. I could tell she didn't care for my appreciation.

"Yeah, me neither."

"Given there are fifty states, it will take forever to locate her. Any way you can narrow it down for me?"

She hesitated for a bit and, to my surprise, said, "Maine."

"Maine? Excellent. Emily, you've been most helpful, and I appreciate that." Armed with new knowledge, I turned around and headed to my room to change my clothes and start the day.

I promised Drew I'd take one more trip to Diamond Head and check the place out in case I had overlooked something. The trip to Hawaii was long and tedious, and I wouldn't let this opportunity slide by. I might as well go out and investigate while I was here. I headed through the open hotel lobby door and looked to my left, then to my right, and headed on the curbside along the beach. The ocean was turbulent; I saw a large cargo ship in a distance. Near the shore were a few surfers getting ready to tackle the waves.

As I turned left at the street fork, the ocean disappeared from my sight and the sun was beating down. A woman and a girl walked toward the park hand in hand. The girl carried a backpack, and she didn't look happy. She must have headed to school, and she probably hated it.

Diamond Head was around the corner, and the uphill path was getting steeper. I turned around to check out what I had already walked and in the corner of my eye, on the other side of the street, I saw the man. The one who had been following me. His ponytail was down. Even so, with his large stature and confident moustache, I knew it was him.

I stopped in my tracks and turned toward him forcefully so he could tell I knew about his intentions. When the street was empty, I crossed it, and I found myself in front of the man. He looked at me, somewhat puzzled, and said, "May I help you, sir?"

"You son of a bitch!" I advanced my fist toward his face, and he raised both his arms in self-defense.

I jabbed him in his stomach, and he yelped once and bent down slightly.

"What, what are you doing?" I grabbed one of his arms and twisted it as hard as I could, and he screamed. "Ahhhhhh." He wrestled, trying to get out of my armlock, but he was having a hard time getting out of it.

I was quite out of breath when I stopped attacking, and my eyes were now locked with his.

"Why are you following me?" I said with my teeth clenched. I was annoyed and confused. He seemed almost harmless from this distance. His eyes were tamed, and he seemed troubled.

"Following you? What are you talking about? I don't even know who you are."

"I saw you last night at Moana Surfrider Hotel. You stared at me half the night. Who sent you?"

He put his head down, and his eyes glittered with sadness. "No one sent me. I don't know you. Let me go."

"I don't believe you." I gave him a couple of shakes, but he didn't seem to be fazed. "What is your name?"

"Andrew Golub."

"Andrew Golub, speak up and tell me who sent you. Why are you following me?" But the man said nothing and only shrugged. I looked at him a little closer and noticed his jaw wasn't pronounced like I remembered it from last night. Did I catch the wrong man and wrongly accused him? "Okay, Andrew Golub. I'll let you go now, but if I see you again, you'll be in trouble. Hear me?"

He nodded and gave me a quick smile. There was no trace of evil in this man as I kept examining him.

"And by the way, 'golub' means 'pigeon' in Serbo-Croatian. Don't ask how I know this."

The man didn't want to engage further and just walked away in the same line he walked before. I just stood there and watched him become smaller and smaller. Me, I felt like a jackass. I attacked the wrong man. I continued on my trip to Diamond Head, hoping it would be luckier this time around. When I arrived, I rummaged through the rocks. The ones I could lift hid nothing under. The rocks produced zero diamonds. At that point, I was sure that Drew and I had to talk to Ursula more. Or give up the entire mission.

I lay on a large rock and a single tear came down my check, ending in my ear. I wiped it for it tickled me. My defeat was materialized. My hope plunged. I believed the diamonds were out of reach or had already been discovered. It was time to return home and reinvent my life, maybe find a job, be a mediocre man, settle for less.

There was only one thing that could make me feel better. Writing another letter to Lillian.

*Dear Lillian,*

*I am delighted to have found you and be able to compose these letters to you. Ever since I laid my eyes on you, I must admit you cross my mind often. I'd love to get to know you better, as a person, to know what makes you tick, what your strength and weaknesses are, what makes you happy, sad, angry... There's nothing better than having a soulmate to whom you can confess all your secrets, say everything that's on your heart and mind. As time goes by, I hope to become that person for you, and you for me.*

*Here's something I want to tell you: I used to be married. My wife, Barbara—whom I affectionately called Barb—and I met in college. She was a psychology major, while I was a computer science major. We met in the drama class, and I remember how bright and joyful she always seemed. We got paired to perform Romeo and Juliet that semester and ended up getting together in evenings to learn our lines and rehearse. Because of her presence, I was too nervous and I couldn't concentrate, so I was messing up my lines all the time. Instead of getting irritated, she laughed, and her laughter was loud and infectious. Her teeth were like pearls; her long hair enveloped her beautiful round face, and I fell in love.*

*I had had girlfriends before Barb, but they were not serious relationships. None of them made me feel like*

*Barb did. A man wants to feel free in a woman's life so he can provide for her and the family. A man seeks a woman who will complete him, not make him feel incompetent or bad. Whenever I made a mistake, I'd hate myself for it. Sometimes, I'd grunt and punch the air, and she'd put her hand on my shoulder and say "it's okay, Carl. Don't beat yourself up over this small thing. Life's too short for anger." And just like that, my ill feelings would disappear.*

*After college, we went our separate ways —I went back to my hometown in Ohio, and she to California. But a few years later, at the college reunion, I came across her again. She was the same charming Barb, but more beautiful. Her smile, when I saw her again, disarmed me. We dated shortly after and two years later; I asked her to marry me. We were still in our twenties—young and naïve—but full of life and enthusiasm. We had so many plans together to conquer the world...*

Out of nowhere, I felt something fall on my face, which disrupted my train of thought. Above me flew a pigeon that disposed of its waste on me.

"Son of a gun!" It still felt warm and gooey. Most unfortunately, I had nothing to wipe it with. I took a stone and scraped my face with it. The stone was warm and had sharp edges, so I focused so as not to poke my eye with it. This was definitely Andrew Golub sending his revenge from the gods upon me. But maybe I deserved it.

I stood up and descended into the city. It was a calm day. Feral chickens and roosters roamed freely on the lawns and curbside. As I approached them, they'd slowly move away, unafraid of my presence. I stopped by a local café and grab something to drink.

As I entered, a youngish woman greeted me and asked me what I wanted. I read the menu on the wall behind her and ordered iced coffee.

"Coming out soon, sir."

On the counter, I noticed today's local newspaper Hawaii Post and on the front was an advertisement in large letters:

KUAOLA RANCH TOURS AVAILABLE NOW!
COME AND SEE THE NATURE WONDERS
EXPLORE THE WORLD WAR II BUNKER AND
MORE!
Tour buses leave every 30 minutes

"Can I please take this paper?" The girl behind the counter was taken aback like she had never heard this question before.

"Yeah, sure."

I took a few paper bills out of my pocket and handed them to the girl. "Keep the change."

My legs moved as fast as possible. When I arrived at the hotel, I walked up to the reception, where Emily looked busy typing on her personal computer. I approached her and whispered, afraid to startle her, "Emily."

She lifted her head, "Yes?"

"I need to ask you a question."

"What is it?"

"I need to get to Kuaola Ranch as soon as possible. Can you tell me where it is and how to get there?"

"Oh, yes, sure. I can certainly help with that." She took a map out and spread it on the counter between us. She pointed at the southern part of the map. "We're here right now, and Kuaola Ranch is right here." She moved the finger to the northeast part of the island.

"A local bus can get you there in less than an hour. But you can also rent a car if you want more freedom and explore the other parts of the island."

"Thank you, Emily. As always, you've been so helpful."

It was only nine a.m., and the day was still young. Plenty of time to get to the ranch and explore it. I embarked onto the street right away, delighted at my new discovery, and stuck out my right thumb, hoping to get a ride.

7

A Chrysler minivan pulled over on the shoulder. It moved toward me in reverse and stopped at my feet. A window on the passenger side opened up and a young man, topless with curly blond hair, leaned forward and said, "Where to?"

"Kuaola Ranch."

"Perfect. Hop in." I opened the door and sat in the passenger seat. The minivan was packed with stuff in the back. On each side of the van stuck out a surfing board. At my feet were a volleyball, a duffle bag, snorkeling gear and a pair of old shoes. His car smelled of old socks and rain. "I'm heading to the North Shore. I can drop you off there. It's on the way."

"It's my lucky day," I said.

"You're not from here, are you?"

"No. I'm from Massachusetts. Well, born and raised in Ohio, but been in Mass for a while. You're a local?"

"Yeah. Born and raised in California but been in O'ahu for twenty years. How long are you here for?"

"Just a few days. Leaving tomorrow, most likely." He drifted his gaze from the road to me and looked at me like he was examining me.

"How do you like it here so far?"

"I like it. I like it. No complaints, except for the roosters waking me up early morning." The man laughed loudly, penetrating my ears with the sound traveling in the small space.

"Those darn roosters. You get used to them like you do to everything else. Don't you guys have squirrels back home? Aren't they, like, everywhere?"

"They are, but I don't remember them ever waking me up." He laughed again.

"Good point." He opened his window, and I welcomed the breeze coming from the outside. "Mind if I light a smoke?"

"No, not at all." He took a pack from the glove compartment and lit a cigarette, inhaling smoke deeply like he was meditating.

"One of these days, I'm hoping to quit." He brought the cigarette closer to his face and looked at it as if he was having a conversation with it. "But it's hard to do it when smoking is everywhere. Restaurants, bars, parks, workplace... even if I quit, they say secondhand smoke can kill you. I'd rather kill myself than let someone else kill me."

"I agree, it's unavoidable." As the conversation went on, I thought of Drew and his chain-smoking habit. If Drew only knew where I was heading right now. He'd be pleased, no doubt.

From the city bustle, we got onto the highway, a three-lane road one way. The roads were gently sloping down, then ascending up like gentle giant waves. From the distance stood mountain ranges that changed their form, color, and shapes from different angles as we moved. The valleys beneath were scattered with houses, a rare residential building peeking out. We passed the sign for Pearl Harbor, the place where tourists frequented to get a glimpse of the recent history.

The surroundings were bloomed in lush vegetation. The trees, that I hadn't seen before, were of bright orange and purple. It was pleasing to see the sights. We got onto Route 83, a narrow road with one lane in each direction. As we got closer to the ocean, we could nearly touch it with our arms. That was how close the road was to the water. The beaches were empty. An occasional bicycle rider got in our lane, and the young man, my generous driver, made an arch to avoid hitting them.

"Mind if I play some music?" The young man asked.

"Yeah, no. Go ahead."

The man pulled an audio cassette from the glove compartment and inserted into the cassette slot on the car dashboard. A few seconds later, music played. It was heavy, and I felt the bass beat inside me.

"Have you listened to this album?" The man yelled on top of the music so I could hear him.

"No, who is this?"

"It's Guns 'n' Roses. Their new album *Appetite for Destruction*. Dude, it's friggin' dope. I love it." He sang along loudly. As Welcome to the Jungle blasted through the van, I thought about the ranch. I had no preconceived notion of what it looked like or what to expect. The newspaper clearly spelled out the bunker was part of the ranch. Ursula said nothing about it to Drew, but it was quite possible she didn't trust him with the information. If I had been there, maybe she would have been more willing to reveal. I saw her smiling at me when I went to meet her. She wasn't smiling at Drew. She and I connected. I felt it.

The fact I was close to potential clues made me feel better about the mission. My instincts rarely led me astray. I knew there was a clue waiting somewhere.

The man yelled, "Hey, hey." I turned to him and

he was waving at me. "Dude, are you deaf? We're here."

He pulled over at a large parking lot, and beyond, there appeared a majestic mountain range that was part of the ranch. They looked like green, giant slopes lined up in multiple rows. Against the mountain was the clear blue sky. It was a perfect day to explore.

I bid the young man farewell, and he turned around in his van and crept toward the highway; the music becoming fainter.

I walked through the gift shop and on the other side came up to the ticket booth at which a large man greeted me with "Aloha, and welcome to Kuaola Ranch. How can I help you?"

"I'd like a ticket for the next tour session."

"Absolutely. The bus is leaving in seven minutes." He pointed to the small houses on our left side and told me the bus would pick up the people and leave from there.

I grabbed my ticket and was on my way. On the summit, a couple of horses were walking around with the mountain range in the background. A few people watched their grace and beauty, and the horses walked around slowly, unaware of the people's presence.

The bus looked similar to a yellow school bus, except all the windows were open, and it was green with KUAOLA RANCH TOURS spelled out on the side. Our driver, an older lady with a hat on, wore a small microphone on her T-shirt and ushered us onto the bus. The tour was small—only five of us joined. There was a younger couple with a toddler and a woman who seemed sad or depressed, and perhaps on this journey all alone after a recent breakup. I could only speculate. I sat in the second to last row to better absorb the scenery.

The bus moved and the dust behind us left a cloud. The woman talked about the ranch history, none of which I followed until she mentioned the word 'bunker.' She said something about the land being taken over by the U.S. military in 1941; after the Japanese attacked the Pearl Harbor, the US built this bunker in order to have protection and watch for future attacks. They named it "Battery Cooper" and finished building it in 1943. It sat inside a rock of the ranch, overseeing the ocean and the small islands close to the shore.

The ranch was endless. It sat on a 4,000-acre parcel of land with majestic views of the mountains on one side and the ocean on the other. The green mountains looked like they were painted with rough brush. I could see potential beyond the place giving tours—maybe it could serve as a movie set about dinosaurs or similar. But I digressed.

We made our first stop, and it was the bunker.

She parked next to a rock where the bunker's entrance was several feet away. The driver announced we had only fifteen minutes to explore the place before we headed out again. I rushed to get off the bus since the time was ticking fast against my desires. At the entrance of the bunker was an old, deep green ambulance jeep with the red cross on the side. The heavy metal double doors were wide open and the other people were already inside exploring. I entered, and on the left side, noticed the original map of the bunker. The bunker's shape on the map resembled a W with six short hallways sticking on its sides. There were two storage rooms, one located inside each end of the W.

The walls were made of stone and the ceiling was cut in the arch. Even though it was a bunker, the space was well lit, with several lights on overhead. When I entered the storage room, two rocks three feet by a foot in size were sitting on each side of the room. In between, there were wooden planks inter-woven with each other, making a gate-like with a door and windows appear. I walked into the small space behind the wooden gate and noticed a hole the size of my fist in the wall. I peeked my head to check out the hole, but it was dark and impossible to see inside. I put my hand inside and pulled it out quickly, fearing what I might touch inside. But I compressed my fear and placed my hand into the hole again. The hole kept getting deeper and deeper until my arm to the elbow was swallowed by it. With the tip of my fingers, I could feel something, perhaps a tick leaf or a piece of paper. As the hole was narrow, my fingers struggled to pinch the object at the bottom. I came closer to the wall to allow my arm to reach for more depth. I slowly put the index fingertip on the object, then I moved my thumb to meet the object on the other side. I finally grabbed it and drifted it upward in the fear of losing it or ripping it apart.

A single piece of paper, thick and browned from age, was at the tip of my fingers. I grabbed with my other hand and brought it close to my eyes. A message was written on it I couldn't understand, for it was written in a foreign language.

The note read:

*Wer den schatz sucht, sollte nach Nuremberg gehen. Zeppelin.*

"This looks German," I whispered all to myself.

I didn't speak a word of the language. I dabbled in Spanish once upon a time, but never became fluent. English was the only language I knew and spoke. But I was confident this note led to our clue to the diamonds.

I looked around to make sure no one saw me, even though it was clear the other tourists had already ventured here and left. I placed the piece of paper in a safe place, an inside pocket of my summer vest.

The woman driver's voice traveled through the space. "Fifteen minutes up! Hop on the bus! We're departing now!"

At the bunker's exit, the view of the ocean ahead of me gave me new hope and energy. Everyone on the tour jumped on the bus and we continued on our tour. The driver kept telling stories and offering the history of the place, but I paid her no attention. I was too focused on the note. My curiosity grew with each minute, every inch we moved, and I couldn't wait for the tour to be over. On my right, I saw a line of people riding horses, plodding across the hill. They were having a different tour. The view was breathtaking. If heaven existed, it would certainly look like this, I was sure.

Soon enough, we descended into the summit and the tour was over. The tour lady thanked everyone and asked us to come back. I held the vest pocket tightly with my hand like the most precious possession I had gained. It was my ticket to fortune, to freedom, to a place where all worries would keep at bay. It was still early in the day. I hopped on 83 and hitchhiked in the Honolulu direction. To my surprise, a minibus pulled over, and the driver put the blinking lights on. He stood up from the wheel, walked to the door, peeked his head through. "Going to Honolulu?"

I put my hand down. "Yes, sir."

"Hop on."

I ran to the bus and when I stepped inside it, the wave of heat and humidity took my breath away. I could barely catch the air. There were no passengers in the minibus, which for a second made me feel uneasy. Was I being kidnapped? Would the driver find my note and take it away from me? But the driver, a man around my age, seemed to have minded his own business—as soon as I got on, he put the left blinker on and drove onto the road.

He yelled from the front as if he had no sense for space, "Are you a tourist?"

"Sure am."

"I can tell." He laughed.

"How can you tell?"

"Well, almost no one who lives on the island would ever hitchhike."

"I like to add excitement to my travels," I said jokingly and put my hand on the vest pocket.

We remained silent for the rest of the trip. As we came closer to the city, more asphalt was emerging, and fewer trees were present on the sides of the road. I had to make yet another stop before I went to the hotel. I looked in the driver's direction and found the opportune time to ask him a question.

"Do you know of any bookstores in the city?"

"Bookstore? There's one on the main street. I can drop you off close by. It's on my way to the garage."

We drove a few more minutes before he pulled over and stopped.

"Here. Can't quite drop you off at the front, but if you cross the street and walk another block or two, you will run into a small bookstore. You can't miss it."

"That's kind of you. Do I owe you anything for the ride?"

"No trouble." He waved his arm in dismissal. "Happy to help."

"Mahalo." I thanked him in Hawaiian and exited the bus.

When I crossed the street, my steps quickened and soon enough, I saw the sign.

## ALOHA BOOKSTORE

The lights inside were bright and cheery as if a small sun was shining. The bookstore was small and crowded, with rows upon rows of shelves, all filled with books. It had been a while since I had visited a bookstore and I sought help.

I walked up to a young man with long, greasy hair and thick glasses on his brown eyes and asked him to help me find a German dictionary.

"This way." He walked fast until he stopped at a shelf and bent down to look through a multitude of books. He pulled one out and handed it to me. "I recommend this one."

"Thank you. Is there a place I can sit in privacy and look at it?"

"Oh yeah, sure. Just around the corner, there is a small desk with a chair."

Perfection! I sat down and pulled the note from my vast pocket.

*Wer den schatz sucht, sollte nach Nuremberg gehen. Zeppelin.*

I pored over the pages and flipped them back and forth until I found the words in the book:

*Wer* – who

*Den* – the?

*Schatz* – treasure

*Sucht* – seek

*Solte* – should

*Zu* – to

*Nuremberg*—I didn't need to look this one up, as I had heard of this German town many times before.

*Gehen* – go

*Zeppelin*—wasn't that the field where Hitler gave his big speech?

The words on their own made little sense, but I made sense of them and gathered the message, said:

"Anyone looking for the treasure should go to Nuremberg. Zeppelin." Bingo!

I shut the dictionary down and rushed out of the bookstore, running to my hotel.

As soon as I arrived in my room, I noticed an unwelcomed scene: my luggage had been searched and all my clothes were lying on the floor in disarray. The drawers of the dresser in a corner were wide open. Someone was searching for something valuable in them. This mess was intentional. I stood in one place to assess the situation, feeling disoriented and confused. The only person I could think of that could be the offender of such an act was the man with the ponytail and mustache. He was after the same thing I was, no doubt. But I was yet to discover who he was and how he found out I was after the diamonds.

It was the sign I had to get off the island as soon as possible, and my resolve was to leave the following day.

The phone rang by coincidence, just as I was planning to dial Drew and let him know of my discovery.

"Hello?"

"Hey, Carl. How's it going?"

"Well, I have good news and bad news. Which one do you want to hear first?"

"Start with the bad."

"Someone is still following me and wants our diamonds. I am sure it is the man who appeared in the hotel that time, but I don't know who he is or how he found out we were after the diamonds. You swear you have nothing to do with this?"

"Carl. We went over this already. You know it wouldn't be in my interest to do this to you. Besides, I have never really trusted guys with moustaches." The answer wasn't ideal, but he sounded genuine. "What's the good news?"

"I found the clue to our treasure. Like I suspected, it was hidden in the bunker. I will disclose the location when I come home. In case the phone is wired. I'll be hopping on a plane tomorrow morning."

"Excellent news! You were right about your instincts, Carl. I guess always trust your instincts. Have a safe trip, partner, and see you soon!"

We hung up, and I gathered the clothes and put them in my luggage. Thankfully, nothing was stolen (I guess this person didn't care for my shirts or boxers).

I called the hotel reception and someone answered the phone. "Aloha. Moana Surfrider Hotel. How may I help you?"

"Hi, I wonder if you can help me book a one-way plane ticket to Boston for tomorrow morning?"

"Absolutely, sir. Smoking or non-smoking."

"Definitely non-smoking."

In the morning, I rose early with the sun and the roosters and ordered a cab to the Honolulu airport, a short twenty-minute ride from the hotel. I was closer to home. The diamonds were closer to me. I was closer to a beautiful and carefree life.

## 8

The plane was half empty. My seat was next to the window, and no one sat next to me. I looked forward to the reprieve, a chance to think about our next moves. To sleep a little. To daydream about Lillian and plot ways to find her. I'd write her another letter before I embarked on my journey with her. It was strange to say this, but I loved this woman even though my encounter with her was short-lived. I longed for her, and I hoped our paths would cross again soon.

*Dear Lillian,*

*I'd be remiss if I told you I didn't think of you often. I do. But I've kept busy with important matters lately and haven't finished my previous letter or compose another one.*

*I told you about my wife, Barb. Why was I telling*

*you about her? After almost twenty years of marriage, Barb found she was ill with cancer. The news was devastating, and I was scared. When you live with someone for so many years, you see them as immortal, invincible. But the positive Barb that she was, she tried to comfort me and tell me everything would be alright. Over time, however, she was becoming fragile. Chemotherapy was helping for a while, but it made her thoroughly depressed and hopeless, and she didn't like her hair falling out.*

*Eventually we learned she reached stage IV, and she didn't have much longer to live—a few months at the most. Together, we went through all the phases of the dying cycle—from denial to anger to depression to acceptance—until one morning; I found Barb lying in bed. Her eyes were wide open, and she didn't move. I approached the bed to check up on her, and when I grabbed her hand, she was cold as ice. Her eyes remained silent and motionless. That's when I knew I had lost her.*

*I was married, and I stayed single for a long time after Barb's death. I had dated no one or allowed anyone in my life since. I had been a bit of a recluse, staying at home, busying myself with hobbies, and going out for long walks every day. It's what fulfills me.*

*But ever since I met you—and I hope this doesn't scare you away—you have given me hope I could become attached to another being again. Maybe you'll give me a chance to come closer to you and get to know you better, and vice versa.*

The announcement went off through the plane, "Good afternoon, passengers. This is Captain Miller. We are cruising at a low altitude right now and almost ready to land at the Chicago airport. The local weather is about forty degrees Fahrenheit and the local time is approximately five p.m. We thank you for choosing our airline and we hope to see you soon."

Chicago O'Hare was crowded with people who attempted to get to their gate as quickly as possible. I had about half an hour to my connecting flight and stopped by the newspaper stand to grab today's newspaper. I flipped through the pages and nothing exciting or newsworthy jumped out at me. The world was rolling on as usual.

The Boston flight was on time, and I was happy to be even closer to home. Back home, even in Octo-ber, hints of the winter already beckoned. Much too early, but that was New England. The nights could be cruel and cold, leaving frost bites on grass, rooftops, and the plants in the morning.

Regardless of the weather, I knew I had another important trip ahead of me. Now that the secret note revealed our treasure's location, I hoped this would be my last stop.

On the plane, I made a checklist in my head to prepare for my next trip. Call the travel agency. Meet with Drew. Possibly meet with Ursula. But what could she offer at this point? Her limited direction was confusing, inaccurate, plain wrong. I'd give myself a couple of days to regain my balance and recover from jetlag. I couldn't believe I'd be traveling to the opposite side of the planet within less than a week. How good could that be for one's body? Drink lots of water, someone once said when I was younger and wanted to travel around the world. It would keep me energized, they said.

On the Boston plane, a young woman struggled to keep her wailing baby quiet. The baby must have been in pain. When the baby cried, it would lull me to sleep. I closed my eyes and entered a dreamland. Still fresh from my Hawaii trip, I dreamt about the ocean and a gigantic wave carrying me around. Waves kept moving and getting bigger and bigger while I lay on my back and moved along with them calmly and peacefully. On the shore, I saw people with the hands up on their forehead as if focusing on a distance, checking me out perhaps to see what I was doing, whether I would survive the waves. They looked at each other in confusion and waited a minute or two more to see what I was or what would transpire from riding the wave. I smiled. It was a beautiful ride. When the people on the shore realized I was having fun and not in obvious danger, they turned around and walked away.

I felt a couple of pokes on my left shoulder and opened my eyes.

"We have arrived in Boston, sir."

A young flight attendant stood next to me, smelling of a sweet perfume scent. I appeared to be the only passenger on the plane. I thanked her, grabbed my luggage in the overhead compartment bin, and exited the plane.

The cold air hit me as a surprise when I exited the airport. It was difficult after enjoying the beautiful Hawaii weather. The airport was bustling with taxis. One was easy to hail. The trip to my apartment was tedious. During our ride, the taxi driver was quiet. It took nearly an hour to arrive at my apartment. The only thing he said was the cost of the ride.

"Seventeen." I handed him a twenty-dollar bill and told him to keep the change. My building looked quiet and deserted. I looked up at my apartment windows and they were black. I wondered if Drew was home. Despite that, I'd wait until the morning to see him. A good night's sleep would do me good. As soon as I entered the apartment, the stale smell washed over me. I rushed to open the windows to get some fresh air in, even though the evening was raw. It felt good. There was a lot to do over the next couple of days. I was excited that my future was shaping up, finally.

* * *

The morning came, and I felt a bit disoriented. I had expected to hear roosters outside, but only mourning doves were calling each other in the nearby park. The ticking sound of the grandfather clock in my hallway filled the room. Otherwise, it was quiet, like in a ghost town. I made myself tea and then walk to the lobby to get my mail. My kitchen looked untouched, some dirty mugs still sitting in the sink.

When tea was done, I sat on the couch and thought of Lillian. It was time to look for her. I grabbed the telephone book and skipped pages to Maine. My eyes were anxious as they scanned for the last names that started with a D. But there was no one named Lillian Daisy in the book. I looked again more carefully. Maybe earliness of the morning had me skip the words. But when I double checked, nothing turned up. Could Emily have fooled me? Did she lie to me about Lillian's name just to get me off her back? Regardless, I was determined to find her. I would find a way. Meanwhile, another letter popped into my head and I crafted it.

*Dear Lillian,*

*I am back home from Hawaii, and for the first time in a while, I feel lonely. Meeting you has made me think what it would be like to have a lifetime partner I'd enjoy* spending time with and sharing precious moments. I just tried looking you up in the phone book, but no name by Lillian Daisy appears there. I will take my time to find you, even if that means visiting Maine and driving town to town. Yes, the task seems implausible, but miracles have happened.

As I sit here on my couch, the smell of my tea brings me back to my childhood. I'd like to tell you about it, so you know a little more about me.

I grew up in Ohio, in a small town near Dayton. I was born in the dead of the winter. Apparently, the day I came to the world, the snow was high and my parents couldn't transport me home, so they kept me in the hospital for an additional few days. When they brought me home, they had a party where everyone in our extended family showed up.

I have vague memories of my mother when I was little. Through a fog, I recall her picking me up and giving me smooches on my cheeks. I remember her singing often, and as a child thought she had the most beautiful voice on this living earth. Every day, when my dad came home, food would be served on the table, and we'd sit around and eat in silence. Our home was quite modest. My father was the breadwinner and was the only source of income for the household. My mother was a stay-at-home mom. She cooked, washed our laundry, knitted, crocheted, you-name-it.

When I was four years old, my mother was in a

*terrible car accident, and she didn't survive. I remember that day clearly. My father sat at the kitchen table and sobbed. The house felt empty without her. If it wasn't clear before, it was clear then that she was the pillar of our nuclear family. My dad sat me down that day and explained that Mother flew to heaven and I'd meet her again. I asked him when, but he said he didn't know.*

*I can't remember if I cried or not. But as time went by, I was feeling the gap in the absence of my mother. I felt a piece of me was missing. When I felt sad, she wasn't there to comfort me or pick me up. Eventually, maybe I was five at that point, a woman started to come by our house and my dad would tell me to go to my room and lock myself in. I'd hear them giggling and laughing through the walls. My father would play jazzy music on vinyl and the woman would shout my dad's name until she stopped.*

I spilled tea on myself, and it hurt. "Ouch. Damn it!" I stood up and ran to the kitchen to put some ice on my burned hand.

When my hand felt better, I slipped into sweatpants and sweatshirt and headed down to get my mail. The building hallway was dark and quiet. There were no sounds coming from anywhere. It felt apocalyptic and strange.

At the bottom of the stairs, I noticed a pile of folded newspapers and assumed they were mine accumulated during my trip in Hawaii. I bent down to look at the name of the recipient, but these weren't mine. Did someone collect my newspaper while I was away?

As I propped myself up, I heard someone coming from behind. I could sense the subtle presence of another human being. When I turned around, Drew stood there in his postal uniform and a bag across one of his shoulders. At the encounter with my partner, I gasped, happy to see him, "Hey, Drew!"

"Hello?" He sounded subdued, as if he was too busy sorting the mail in the mailboxes and didn't want to be bothered at the moment.

"So good to see you. I didn't think you were up already."

"What? I am a mailman. I deliver mail. That's what I do."

"Of course. But I thought you usually do your rounds in the afternoon."

"Now, why would you think that?"

"You told me once?" I said, trying to reassure him I wasn't dreaming.

"I am sorry. I barely know you, and we have spoken maybe once or twice before."

Whatever.

"Drew, so..." I whispered. "Come upstairs so I can show you the note I found in the bunker."

"Huh?"

"The note. You already forgot?"

"I am sorry. But I really don't know what you're talking about." He moved his head away in the opposite direction and carefully sorted the mail before he put them in the individual mail slots.

"Drew. The note for the diamond location. We're going to be rich."

Drew jerked his head in my direction and gave me the look with the eyes as big as a house.

"What the hell are you talking about?"

"Diamonds! We're going to be rich, Drew. Our dream is coming true finally."

"I'm sorry. But I am busy here sorting the mail." He turned in the opposite direction again and seemed to have ignored me.

I stood there and waited for Drew to change his attitude. It was entirely possible he didn't want to discuss the diamond matters with me while he was working or in public. Maybe he wanted privacy. Maybe he was too tired and didn't have enough head space to discuss these matters.

"Drew. Listen. Come to my place after you drop all the mail, and we will discuss our next steps. Okay? You must see the note. We have the correct location at last. Have you seen Ursula lately?"

"Ursula? Why the hell would I want to see Ursula?"

"Why not? You could have asked her more questions. Or visit her, so we're less suspect."

"Suspect? I don't know what the hell your problem is. You've lost your mind." Drew's voice sounded annoyed and harsh.

"I know this is too much to take, partner, but you'll be happy when things are sorted out and the diamonds are in our possession."

Drew approached me and brought his face close to mine. He clenched his teeth and spoke through them with obvious anger.

"Listen, you lunatic. Leave me the hell alone. I am working. If you keep harassing me with this bullshit, I'll smash your face." I looked at his mouth, his lips barely moving, as saliva flew out through them. Drew simply lost it.

I thought it was him who had lost his mind. I needed to get him back and continued on with our mission. He was probably overwhelmed and stressed out and needed some time to process the fact that he would become rich soon. It wasn't a slight change in life, going from an ordinary mailman to a rich guy. His lifestyle would completely change. He wouldn't need to worry ever again.

"Take it easy, Drew. I need to know what is going on with you."

"Nothing is going with me, and I think you need to leave me alone." Drew's tongue was as sharp as his look.

"Drew!" I screamed. "What the fuck is going on? You better listen! Listen to me for once, for crying out loud! We are going to be rich soon, and I need you to stick with the plan." I was pounding my fist against the palm of my hand.

Drew stood there, steaming. "Leave. Me. Alone, you crazy fuck."

We stared at each other for a while until I walked away.

Drew would soon return to his old self. I felt that. Then we could resume our mission and we'd reach the diamonds in no time.

**9**

———————

K nock knock.

Someone knocked on my door. It was an early afternoon, the day I returned from my trip to Hawaii. Who could it be? I approached the door and looked through the peephole. Drew stood there, showing his profile. Ah, Drew. He was probably here to check out the note and plan for my trip to Germany. I opened the door, and he turned his head toward me.

"Hey, Carl!" He looked happy to see me. I was glad he came around. "I'm so happy to see you, partner. May I come in?"

"May you come in? Of course! We have a lot to talk about."

Drew entered my apartment and went for the sofa, sat down and put his feet on the coffee table.

He crossed his arms and put them behind his head, forming an armrest.

"Can I get you something to drink?" I said.

"I'm good. I'm here to see the miracle of the note you found. Show me."

I walked away to grab the note and when I returned, Drew was leaning forward on the sofa, anticipating the moment of truth.

"Here it is." I handed him the piece of paper and he took it ever so gently to not destroy it. He placed it on the table and studied it.

"Wow. It's in German. I studied German in high school. The note said that whoever seeks the treasure should go to Nuremberg. Zeppelin."

"Very good. I'm glad we agree on that." I smiled at Drew.

"So, what's next?" He leaned back on the sofa.

"I'm on my way to Germany in a couple of days. I need to call the travel agency and book a plane ticket today. I hope that I find the secret place right away and return with the diamonds. There's one thing I'd like to do before I leave, though. I'd like to visit Ursula and find out if she remembers anything about Zeppelin. Of course, I know she has dementia, but sometimes mind can trick. So, what do you say? Do you want to come visit Ursula with me? Tomorrow morning?"

"Sure, partner. Whatever you want."

When Drew left my place, I called the travel agency and booked a ticket. The same woman who booked my ticket to Hawaii answered the call. When she recognized my name, she exclaimed, "Oh, sir, you travel so much! You should sign up for our benefit program. For every three round-trip tickets, you get one free."

"Thank you, but I don't think that will be necessary. I don't plan on traveling much after this trip. Maybe only to Maine. And I won't be flying."

"Great, sir. Your ticket will be ready tomorrow morning. Please let us know if there is anything we can do for you."

"Ah yes. I think I need something else while I'm there."

"What is it, sir?"

"I need to rent a car. I'll be driving from Munich to Nuremberg."

"We can help with that, sir. Any brand that you prefer?"

I paused and thought about it. "How about a Mercedes-Benz?"

The woman smiled charmingly. "Of course, Mr. Walker. That's the right choice in Germany. Once your car is booked, I will have that information along with the plane ticket."

We hung up, and I was on my way for a walk. The neighborhood looked glum with an impending winter. People already seemed to have hunkered down, as the streets were bare. I stopped by the café and Anna greeted me with a worried look on her face.

"Carl! Where have you been? It's so unlike you to not stop by three days in a row."

"Good morning." I greeted her and put a smile on my face to immediately ease her concerns. "I was traveling."

"Oh. How adventurous of you. How far?"

"All the way to Hawaii."

"Hawaii? I always wanted to go there." She placed a muffin and a cup of coffee on the counter as if they both waited for me to arrive. "What did you do in Hawaii?"

"I got bored here at home, so I checked out the islands."

Anna smiled. "It is so good to see you, Carl. I was worried, you know. Next time, give me a heads up when you're leaving town."

"In fact, I am leaving for Germany in a couple of days."

"You are? Whereabouts?"

"Munich, then Nuremberg."

"I have a cousin who lives in Munich. His name is Rolf. Let me give you his home address and local telephone number so you can check him out." She turned around and bent down on the counter, writing a note. She handed me a piece of paper with the address and phone number written and said, "If you ever need anything, call Rolf. Even if you just want to grab coffee, he'll be up for it." She waved her arm as if to say it wasn't a big deal.

"Will do. Thank you, Anna." I put the note in my pocket and found my way out.

The following morning, bright and early, I knocked on Drew's door. He opened the door and was all dressed up and ready to face Ursula.

"Good morning, Carl. I thought about it last night and realized you were a genius. It's amazing you found that note that gave us the diamond location."

"Well..." I felt flattered. "Like I said, I am thankful for my instincts. Let's see if Ursula can confirm it for us. I'm nervous, truth be told."

"Listen, Carl. No need to be nervous. Even if she doesn't give us any clues, we still know where the diamonds are located. We're cool." He winked at me and exited through the door.

We strolled down the hall until we approached Ursula's door. We heard the radio on the other side, loud. She seemed to have been listening to the news. We used the doorbell this time, because we weren't sure she'd hear a knock. A minute later, she stood at the door with a tired look on her face.

"You're here again. Come on in." We looked at

each other, shrugged and entered her apartment. She approached the radio and turned down the volume. "What brings you here today, gentlemen?"

"We wanted to say hello and see how you've been."

She looked around her apartment as if disoriented and said, "Fine. How am I supposed to be?"

"Fine is good," Drew said. He turned to Carl and said, "Carl just returned from Hawaii. He had a really enjoyable time there. It was sunny all the time, and people are hospitable. Ever been?"

"Hawaii? What the hell would I do in Hawaii? It's too far."

"True. But Carl will tell you it's worth it. And now he's planning a trip to Germany. Your home country."

She looked at Drew, then shot a gaze at me and kept staring.

"What are you gonna do in Germany?"

"I'm going to visit the Zeppelin field." Her eyes widened.

"The Zeppelin field? I was there in 1945."

"You were?" Both Drew and I leaned forward to listen carefully.

"Yah. I don't remember why I was there, but I was. I think there was someone else there with me, and I don't remember what he was doing there. Everyone said Germany lost the war as the war was about to end. People around us fled to Argentina, Brazil, and other parts of the world. I think a lot of them were guilty of the genocide and tried to run away."

"You seem to remember a lot, though."

"Yah. But I don't remember what I did yesterday. Or who exactly you are. I think I've seen you around before."

"We're your neighbors. We promised to stop by to check up on you every once in a while."

"Yah. That's right." She seemed to have remembered. "Are you looking for the diamonds?"

I gulped. Drew stuttered like a scared and lost kid.

"D-d-diamonds? You do remember the diamonds?" Drew asked.

"Of course, I remember the diamonds. General Mayer placed them in the secret place while in total panic. He was about to flee Germany. But I don't remember if that was on the Zeppelin field." She looked to the side and seemed to think hard. She lowered her voice as if she talked to herself. "I don't know where he went or whether he survived. But anyway," her voice returned to normal. "The diamond secret is not such a secret. Several people tried to find it, but they all ended up dead."

"Dead?" Drew inquired.

"Yah. Dead. There's a man who hunts them

down and kills them. He knows about the secret place, and he won't let anyone near it."

"Who is this man? What's his name?"

"I don't know exactly. But he is quite nasty and has no remorse for killing."

"How do you know all this?"

"I can't tell you, but if my memory serves me, it's all true. If you're going to get those diamonds, I wish you luck."

"How come you never tried?"

"Not interested. I like to live a simple life. Diamonds are not my thing. Plus, I'd never return to Germany ever again. Dreadful memories."

"I understand. Any last-minute advice for us?"

She paused and looked at us both, trying to think of anything wise she could muster. "Yah. If you're gonna go after them, try not to get killed. They are out there up for grabs. But so are bad people."

"Why do you think the diamonds are still left untouched?" I was growing more curious as Ursula revealed more information.

"Because no one got lucky to find the exact location so far. Everyone knows the Zeppelin field, but Jesus, the field is enormous. You'll spend at least a few days searching." My heart sank. The mission seemed closer but more impossible at the same time. And what if someone tried to kill me? A possible case scenario. I'd have to be ready.

"So, tell me. If you knew all this, why did you send me to Hawaii, why not Germany right away?"

"Why not? You said it was a nice place."

"I guess I did. It was worth it." I offered a smile and stood up from the couch. "I have a lot to do today. You've been very helpful, and I thank you." I bowed toward Ursula and she just stared at me.

"Yah," she finally said. Drew followed me and we both were on our way out.

"Phew," Drew said.

"I guess the good news is Ursula remembers the important details and the diamonds are where we think they are. But the bad news is I might get killed during my treasure hunt."

"We hope for the best, Carl." Drew nodded at me.

"Easy for you to say."

"One thing you can do to minimize that chance is to go at night and bring a weapon with you. Just in case."

"Thanks for helping me strategize. Any other brilliant ideas you've got?"

"Hey, hey. You're getting a little mean. I'm just trying to keep you alive."

"Oh thanks. But I guess you're right. I need to be ready and alert and the best time to go hunting will be at night."

"You see." Drew lit up.

We parted ways, and I was on my way to the travel agency. The same woman greeted me with the same cheer. "Mr. Walker, good afternoon. Your trip is all set." She handed me a hefty envelope and continued, "Here's your one-way ticket to Munich and information for the rental car. I hope you have a safe trip."

On my way home, I stopped by a small bookstore where I sought books on World War II. The topic fascinated me, and I still couldn't fathom the killings and tortures that took place only a few decades earlier. For Hitler to rise to such power and cause destruction, organize crimes and killings via concentration camps, occupy so many countries that were helpless and hopeless seemed like a modern history phenomenon. How could humankind prevent these atrocities in the future? How did we learn from history?

It took only one man, an insane man certainly, to cause global upheaval and disruption. Think of the Holocaust. A serial killing of innocent people because of some crazy preconceived notion about Jews being inferior and should disappear from the face of the Earth. Crazy motherfucker. Hitler was. And crazier were even those who followed him like sheep and believed in his ideologies. Did they wake up every morning and thought to themselves, Yeah, Hitler is right! I am superior to everyone else. No one else should occupy this planet except me and my kind. Let me kill everybody else who doesn't fit the mold. I will become an expert killer and fulfill my leader's desires.

Then they slaughtered. Without remorse.

I was lost in my thoughts when someone came from behind. "Sir, can I help you?"

I told the salesperson I was looking for books on World War II and he offered me an array of books on the topic. "Of course, they're all so different, but you won't go wrong with any."

I settled for one, paid for it, and was on my way.

At home, I packed up a duffel bag and placed the note Anna gave me in a side pocket. I'd perhaps need her cousin Rolf. In the evening, I went to bed early, as I had to get up early to catch my flight. But the jitters were getting the best of me, and I couldn't close my eyes to get into the dreamland.

Lillian came to mind, and I had an urgent desire to compose her another letter.

*Dear Lillian,*

*I've been busy lately and haven't looked for you further. I promise to do that as soon as I free my time up and I have nothing else on my calendar. I think of you often; your bright face, your beautiful smile, your silky hair are the highlight of my day when they cross my mind. Trust me.*

*Before I find out, my goal is to tell you more about*

my childhood. When my father started dating a woman after my mother's passing, he changed. Not for the better certainly. For much, much worse. His new lady, whose name was a mystery, because my dad called her different names all the time, was much younger than my mom. She was busty and had a small waist. I remember her wearing low-cut blouses and miniskirts with high heels all the time, and whenever I was in presence of the two of them, my father would constantly stare at her. She laughed all the time, but she was also extremely moody when things didn't go her way. My father would appease her every time she had a tantrum, then things would calm down.

She barely ever paid me attention. Once or twice, she'd come up to me and run her index finger on my cheek, but she never picked me up to give me a hug and a smooch like my mother once did. It was at these times that I painfully missed my mother more than anything in the world.

Because this woman seemed to take over my father's life, I was nearly invisible. Sometimes, he'd come home late and go to bed as soon as he crossed the door, and sometimes, when he brought her home, he'd tell me to go to my room and lock myself in. And not to come out until he told me so.

My room was small, like a place that belonged to young boys. There was a single bed in one corner, a *dresser next to it, and a wooden chair that was wobbly and never used.*

*My choices doing things while being locked alone in the room were limited. I could go to bed and cry my eyes out, missing my mom, or I could play with my toys. On the dresser, I had a scarce number of dolls and teddy bears I got for my prior birthdays. When my mother died, gifts stopped coming. I had to be happy with what I had.*

I heard the ambulance sirens outside, and I wondered if anyone was in grave danger. I hoped not. With that thought, my eyes closed, and a strange sense of tiredness lulled me to sleep.

The following day, bright and early, I was on my way to the airport. It felt like déjà vu all over again. A cab came, picked me up, drove me to the airport. At the gate, I pulled the book and read until they called for boarding. I showed my passport and my boarding pass and found my window seat on the plane. A young man sat next to me then realized he made a mistake then found his seat. The plane was half full. It was a good sign. I would get my sleep and be ready for the treasure hunt at night.

It was a direct flight from Boston to Munich. The pilot said it was seven and a half hours long. The minutes stretched into hours and time was a slow ticking clock. We flew into a morning and the dark clouds were quickly becoming bright white spots in the sky. The sun was also somewhere on the horizon, peeking through occasional clouds, a reminder that the Earth was indeed round.

On the sides of the plane, I could see cigarette smoke traveling through the aisles. The cigarette smell was permanently attached to the chairs and everything else that the plane was made of. It was inescapable.

A loud scream of a woman traveled on the plane. Then a man screamed along and their terrorizing voices filled the plane. What was happening? The screams wouldn't stop. I stood up from my seat to see what the commotion was all about, and several rows ahead of me, a medium-sized man was pointing at the screaming woman. He had a knife in his hand and yelled out "Shut up, shut up, bitch!"

The screaming man next to the woman held her from behind and tried to reason with the man with the knife. "No! Don't do it! Don't hurt her! Don't hurt us."

The man lifted his arm up in the air and the knife shone bright against the airplane lights projecting from the ceiling. "You shut up too. I'm gonna kill you both!"

The man with the knife turned around and ran toward the EXIT door. Wait, what was he doing? He reached for the door and strained to open it. His body moved back and forth as he tried to bolt, the door opened, but, luckily, the door didn't budge.

It occurred to me the man tried to kill us all. Was this a terrorist attack? Or an attack of a man with no sanity? Why would he want us all killed? Who was he? I was ready to face my death. Paralyzed, I watched him grab the door and yank it as hard as he could. The door still didn't move, but the man was determined, like it was his life's mission. In a split second, my life flashed in front of my eyes—a dot of time I had spent on this planet seemed like a miniature saga story. Nothing major to see. Before I said goodbye to all my memories, good and bad, a loud voice, louder than any, screamed, "Freeze!"

A man, looking ordinary with a plaid shirt and a baseball hat, approached the crazy man and grabbed his arms, entangling him behind his back. He pulled a Taser from his side pocket and jammed it into the man's buttock. The man screamed and fell down to the floor like a leaf falling from a tree.

Half terrified, half relieved, I exclaimed "Yes" and clapped. The rest of the crowd followed suit. People were cheering and looking frightened. The man with the Taser turned out to be an air marshal. Who knew that they were sitting on the plane in disguise, just like anyone else? They observed us and detected any signs of foul behavior.

I looked down at my hands, and they were visibly shaking. Embarrassed, I grabbed one hand with the other and hid them under my coat. Thankfully, no one saw me. The trip was weird, and I wondered if this was the sign of worse things to come. Ursula said I could be killed. That was the ultimate unacceptable outcome. But I refused to think bad things would happen. I was a man of faith and hope.

I distracted my mind with my new book. The airplane was relatively calm again except for the engines roaring. They took the man to the front of the plane with his hands placed behind his back and handcuffed. It was one way to ensure he could no longer maneuver another potentially mischievous plot.

The flight attendants turned off the lights. Silence occurred. I turned the overhead lights on and got immersed in the book.

As I advanced through the pages, I had a shocking discovery about the Nazis. They used drugs—yes, drugs—in order to elevate their energy and fight in battles. They took cocaine and opiates, but their must-do daily rations were crystal meth. Ordered by the Third Reich, the soldiers were to be awake and alert for hours at a time and advance to the front lines in different parts of Europe. That was how they quickly occupied France and other strategic places.

Crazy that drugs had such power over the human body and mind. Even Hitler himself was on a daily dosage prescribed by his doctor. His already clouded mind was getting more messed up and cloudier. His urge for drugs daily made him an addict; he was getting more ill by the day and his health deteriorated until he completely lost his reasoning.

It made me wonder what would have happened if drugs hadn't played a role during the war at all. Would the Nazis have advanced as far as they had?

My suspicion grew, as I wondered if drugs were to blame for human downfall, and now the genocide too.

Those Germans were crafty and clever. I wondered where General Mayer ended up burying the diamonds. How long would it take me to find the location and unearth them? I could be there for days, for all I knew. But I'd trust my instincts again.

I closed the book to rest and then my eyes.

*Dear Lillian,*

*My favorite toy was a stuffed clown I named Ned. The doll was limp, its head dropping on a side all the time. If I wanted to see its face, I'd prop its head right back up and I would see his sad eyes, red round nose, and big lips. He was a clown, like any ordinary one, but he grew on me, and I was becoming attached to it.*

*When my father locked me in my room, Ned and I would have our tea and then we would talk about all kinds of things to no end. He was super chatty; he liked to tell me about his day at work and all the people he encountered. Sometimes, when things got rough at work, he'd simply apologize and let me know he needed peace and quiet, and I'd let him rest and have his space.*

*But Molly came to the rescue when Ned was busy in his thoughts. Molly was a friend of ours that was nosy and couldn't keep her mouth shut sometimes. Her dress was dirty, her hair in disarray, and she was missing underwear. When she sat on the floor, I'd try not to look in her direction out of shame. But Ned and Molly were always there, no matter what. Although they differed from each other, they both brought me joy and companionship. Sometimes, I'd sneak out of my room and go to the kitchen to steal some food for us, and when I returned, they'd be all worried that my father would catch me and scream at me. When I returned to the room harmless, they'd laugh, and we'd have our snack.*

I felt the plane descending and my ears felt the pressure. We were almost there. The captain announced our soon arrival, both in English and German, and I grew excited that I would set foot on the ground soon. Another long flight did me in. Flying wasn't my favorite, but all would be worthwhile in the end.

Coming out of the Munich airport, the day was almost over, and the city was getting enveloped by darkness. I looked for the signs for rental cars and found the sign for the rental company where my car awaited me. When I arrived, a man with no facial expressions was sitting behind the desk and asked me something in German.

"English?" I said.

"Little English," he responded.

I explained to him I had a car reservation and handed him a piece of paper with the information. He read it carefully and lifted his head, shaking his head slowly.

"Nein. City. You must go to the city."

"What, I can't rent the car at the airport?"

"Nein. City." He wrote something down and handed me a piece of paper. "Here is a street to pick up a car."

I grabbed the piece of paper and walked away. Now, I had to proceed to Plan B. How did I get to my hotel, to the city center? Close to the car rental place, I saw the sign that led to the train station that would take me directly to the city. I looked up the schedule, and the trains were frequent. I came up to the ticket counter and ordered a ticket to Munich.

"Ten Deutch marks," the salesperson said.

"I don't have any Deutch marks." I had just arrived in the country. I forgot to exchange dollars for the German currency. How on earth did I forget? I was annoyed with myself.

"No marks, no ticket," the salesperson persisted.

"I have U.S. dollars. Will you take them, please?"

The salesperson shook her head stubbornly. "No dollars," she insisted.

I put my head down in defeat and considered alternatives. I asked her if there was a currency exchange kiosk at the airport, but she looked at me without blinking or saying a word.

"Listen." I put on my charming hat. "I really need to get to the city. I just came from the United States, and the flight was awful. There was a guy on the plane who tried to open the door while airborne and kill us all. He got caught, but you don't understand—I could be dead right now. I've had a really rough day."

She still stared at me and listened carefully.

"So, please, please, please. Will you let me pay with the U.S. dollars? I will add some extra so you can have it for a beer."

The woman scoffed. "You think every German drinks beer? You stupid Americans."

Ashamed by my comment, I apologized, and she finally caved and put a smile on her face.

"Okay. Okay. I will give you a ticket for U.S. dollars. But know I never do this."

Yeah, I can tell.

"Thank you. I am forever grateful."

"Track five." She lifted her arm and pointed in a right direction. "The train's leaving in two minutes."

I thanked her and was on my way. In exactly two minutes, my train arrived. When I got on, it was long and nearly empty. I sat down on a window seat and across from me sat an older woman with a shawl covering her hair. She seemed sad, depressed; her eyes drooped down on her wrinkled face. She had a scarily empty look in her eyes. I waited for her to meet my eyes so I could acknowledge her presence. When she finally looked at me briefly, I smiled and greeted her in English. I did not know whether she spoke English. In fact, someone told me once that Germans weren't proficient in English. Only a few.

She heard me greet her, but all she did was turn around and mind her own business.

The train was travelling at a good speed. We'd pass old houses, some interestingly burned down like the war had just stopped and the remains of it were showing. I could see side roads in between houses, catching only quick glimpses. The road signs were everywhere, some of which I didn't recognize. I panicked for a second, trying to imagine the disaster in me driving around and deciphering the signs. Maybe the rental car company had a small manual with road sign interpretation. One would hope.

At the corner of my eye, I caught a sign that spelled out: DACHAU. I remembered talks about Dachau in my high school history class when my teacher, Susan Carsen, taught us all about Nazi concentration camps and all the crazy things that took place in them. Almost every male student was in love with Susan Carsen, though. She had gorgeous blonde hair and blue eyes and a body to die for. But she was a kind soul who wanted to impart knowledge, useful knowledge on us. I'd never forget when she gave us a lesson on concentration camps and told us Dachau was among the first ones to open up and was the model for all the others. When she spoke, she took a handkerchief from her pocket and wiped her tears. We never asked her why she was so emotional—did she have any personal losses during World War II? But we loved her for it even more. Later, she had us read Anne Frank's diary and then write an essay about her experiences.

As the train moved at a high speed, so did my thoughts about Susan Carsen. If it hadn't been for her and her kind mannerisms, I'd never learned these tidbits about the war.

The train made several stops, with a few people entering and exiting. As we got closer to the city, the foot traffic thickened. I looked down at my watch and noticed that we had been riding for about thirty minutes. How long was the ride? As my mind raced again, we came to a sudden stop, and I saw a big sign in blue that said MUNICH. This had to be my stop.

I exited the train and found myself in the middle of the train platform, guessing what side to take the exit. The weather was dreary; it seemed like it had rained earlier and the clouds made the darkness bolder and more prominent. I clearly did not know where to go. I went in a direction where the air seemed brighter. I put my duffle bag over the shoulder and quickened my pace. My next step was to find a hotel room; my hope was I would encounter one soon, so I didn't have to wander in the city for a long time. It was getting late. I was tired, and I tripped once, almost falling.

When I entered the center of the city, more people appeared to be around, and that put me at ease. But as I watched them walk, they looked like marionettes wearing their trench coats and hiding their faces behind their caps. For a second, the scene seemed like one from the Twilight Zone, where everyone seemed to be frozen, and I was the only alive being made of blood and flesh.

A bright sign at the end of the narrow road lured me in. I walked up to it and noticed it belonged to a motel with a vacancy. I stopped to look through the window glass and see what it looked like, but the lights were dim and no sign of life seemed to have appeared. What the heck, I'd still check it out.

I opened the door, and like entering through the door of Narnia, the inside seemed completely opposite from what I saw. The lights were happy and bright, and a beautiful woman was standing at the reception desk.

"Willkommen." She placed a smile on her face, revealing the most white and straight teeth I had ever seen. Relieved by the friendliness and hospitality, I informed her I spoke no German.

"Dis is no problem, mister," she said, still smiling. "How can I help you?"

"I'm looking for a room to stay in for a few

nights. Do you have any?"

"Yes. Yes, of course, mister." She handed me a sheet of paper—something like an application to fill out. "Write here and there and I get you a room."

I looked at the "application," and noticed it was all in German. "But I already said I didn't speak German. How do you expect me to fill this out?"

"It's okay, mister. Just fill out your name and you get a room."

I added my name—Carl Walker—on the top of the sheet and handed it back to her. "Here you go."

"Yes, mister." She looked more closely. "Herr Walker."

She walked away without saying a word and I stood there, puzzled by her disappearance. Why would she just walk away? While waiting for her to return, I looked around and noticed different trinkets placed on shelves on the walls. There was a miniature Eiffel Tower, a beer mug, a Guinness glass. On the other shelf were a mini Colosseum, a bull and a matador appearing to fight each other; all these trinkets seemed to be familiar from the places all around Europe until I stumbled upon one I couldn't recognize. It looked like a water fountain in the shape of a gazebo. Several pipes were on the circle. I was stumped. The woman returned, and I gave her no chance to say or do anything. I asked, "What is this here?"

I pointed at the gazebo, and she offered another smile.

"Ay yes. It's a fountain in Yugoslavia. Sarajevo. I went there three years ago for the Winter Olympic Games. This thing is called Sebilj. It was built in 1753. They say if you drink water from the fountain, you'll return to the city."

"And? Did you?"

"Drink water? I wanted to, but the pipes were frozen. It was the middle of the winter."

"Too bad. I hear there's some trouble brewing in that country. Who knows what will become of it? Maybe better to stay put."

She shrugged her shoulders and offered no comments in return.

"Here is your key, Herr. Your room is on the second floor, room number 212."

212. I had the same number room in Hawaii. Could it be a strange coincidence? I thanked her and headed to the room.

When I opened the door, a beautifully decorated room welcomed me. The lavender scent was sweet and inviting. The ceilings were astonishingly high. I sat on the bed and bounced twice to check its firmness. It was just the way I liked it. I placed the duffel bag on the floor next to the bed and lied down.

This night would be a waste. I had no car to get to the Zeppelin field. According to the travel agency, the car rental place was already closed. I'd have to wait until tomorrow to pick up my Mercedes-Benz. Until then, I was held hostage to the room. I could go for a walk, but the mystical nature of the city didn't seem inviting. I turned on the small TV sitting on the dresser and there seemed to be a documentary about Martin Luther. Germans recognized the Reformation Day, October 31, when Martin Luther delivered his ninety-five theses in front of the Castle Church. He apparently chose that day because he knew many people would show up at the church for All Saints day the following day.

The religion didn't interest me, so I switched the channel. There was a repeat of this year's Eurovision, the best song competition among the European countries. A man in a snow-white suit stood calmly on the stage and sang into the microphone. I was too irritated to listen to music, so I turned off the TV.

I lay on my back and crossed my arms at the back of my head and stared at the ceiling. It was way up there. What was the purpose of building places with ceilings this high? Were Germans the tallest people on Earth?

I closed my eyes, and Lillian's beautiful smile crossed my mind. How I longed for her. I wished I could find her and hold her in my arms. But once I was done with this journey, she was my next treasure.

*Dear Lillian,*

*As time went on, I became more distant from my father. He took care of my basic needs. He gave me a bath once or twice a week, and he'd leave food on the kitchen counter for me to take. He had asked our neighbor, Rosetta Wilson, a black lady with a loud voice, to check up on me once in a while. She'd come knocking on our front door every day and when I didn't answer right away, her powerful voice would call my name, "Caaarl." I'd timidly open the door, but she never gave me any reason to fear her. Rosetta had five children, a couple already grown up and moved away from her home.*

*I remember when she heard that my mother died in a car accident; she came to see us and brought chocolate chip cookies. She spoke through her tears and told my dad that if he ever needed anything to let her know. Apparently, she was a stay-at-home mom and only frequented church and her children's school when she dropped them off and picked them up. In the absence of my mother, Rosetta came closest to feeling like a parental figure. Every time she came to visit us, she'd give me a big hug and wouldn't get off me for a long time. Her hugs made me feel good. Sometimes, I'd hope she never let me go or, in a best-case scenario, she'd take me home and keep me. She suggested that to my father, that I come and stay at her house whenever my father was away, but he outright rejected her, like he needed to be in control of my fate.*

*I'd stay in my room most of the time and talk to Ned*

and Molly. Their voices would vibrate through my head, and I'd repeat all the things they'd tell me. They'd remind me they were there for me. Besides Mrs. Wilson, Ned and Molly were the people I could trust and talk to.

A year later, my father's girlfriend left him. I couldn't tell why or what happened between them, but I noticed my father's behavior turn destructive. He'd sometimes stay in bed and refuse to go to work. When I'd come near him, I'd smell alcohol and see a desperate look on his face. When I was that small, I thought when you broke up with someone, a piece of your heart literally breaks off and disappears into your body. I thought then, because my mother had died and now his girlfriend left him, my father's heart fell apart and was half missing.

Once, I approached him to give him a hug, but he pushed me away and I fell on the floor. I came close to the wall and hit my head. The pain throbbed through my skull, and I cried. Instead of picking me up and checking if I was alright, my father yelled at me and tell me I was a naughty child. He told me to go to my room and never come out. I hyperventilated and couldn't catch a breath as I sat on my bed. Ned and Molly stared at me in disbelief and I felt they wanted to say something, but words seemed to have escaped them. My father was a different man. I yearned for my mother like a fish yearned for water. But a little voice inside my head was telling me to hang on. Things would get better, and I would no longer be alone.

## 11

Today was the day. I woke up in my high ceiling room and jumped out of bed like it was on fire. I put on a pair of jeans and a T-shirt and my hiking boots. The day was damp, and the fog enveloped the city. It had to clear before I headed out to the field. It was getting dark early—around 4 p.m.—and it was a relief to know I had enough time to prepare and get to the field. First, I went downstairs to the dining area and ordered myself a hearty breakfast. There were scrambled eggs, accompanied with sausages, and slices of sourdough bread. The smell of the food was making my stomach growl. A waitress came over and offered coffee or tea. I told her I'd like tea, please. Mint.

With food in my stomach, I was ready to tackle the day. First order of business was picking up a rental car. The car rental place, according to the city map, was a few blocks from the motel. I came out of the motel carrying the map in my hand. I knew it would come in handy.

Now that I was out and about in a daylight, people carried a worrisome look on their faces. I wondered what troubled them. No one was smiling. I turned to my right and saw a big church with bells dominating the square. On my left were old houses with windowsills filled with empty flowerpots. Whatever was left of plants must have died with the change of seasons. My gut was telling to take a right and continue on for a few blocks. I looked at the map again and realized I was going in the direction that would take me to the car rental place.

Soon enough, I saw the sign. I had arrived. Inside, a man tall with dark features greeted me and said something in German.

"No German," I said.

"Okay," he said. "I speak English."

Although we could communicate, I said nothing but gave him the piece of paper with the car rental confirmation. He read it and said, "A-ha. Mercedes Benz. Good choice."

He showed me with his hand to follow him and I moved swiftly as he disappeared from behind the wall corner.

We walked into a large parking space where row

upon row of cars of different brands were parked. He confidently walked to a car that had the famous circle with three pointed stars in the center. It was a black, long and boxy-looking 260E sedan.

"Here." He opened the door and showed me in. "This is your car. It's a manual transmission, only five thousand kilometers on the odometer."

"Fantastic." I sat down and put my hands on the steering wheel. "It just feels so great." I looked at my rep and his face remained stiff and serious.

"I have a question, though. Do you have a manual with all the road signs? You know… to show what they mean?"

"Nein. We do not have the manual. We just assume everybody knows how to drive. If you feel uncomfortable driving, you should not."

"Oh, no no no. It was a mere suggestion. I know my signs." I waved my hand and placed it back on the wheel.

"Fine. Now you need to sign the paperwork. Follow me."

I got out of the car and followed him back to the office. There, he pulled a long piece of paper with a small print, all in German. He pointed at the line at the bottom and asked me to sign there.

"Hopefully, I'm not giving my life away." I laughed, but the man remained unmoved.

"I need to know when you will return the car," he asked with the stiff face.

"Do I need to tell you now? Because I don't know when." In my mind, I was thinking it all depended how my treasure hunt went. I could luck out in the first shot and walk away with the diamonds tonight, or I could be stuck with the mission and go back several times until I found the location. And by some crazy luck, I could also end up dead. But I'd rather not think of that possibility.

"You come back here every day and tell us if you return the car."

"Every day?" Some weird car rental system in Germany.

"If you do not know when you will return the car, you will need to keep us updated."

I paused to think if there was a way around this, but I couldn't think of anything. The rental place was close enough to the motel I could walk.

"Can I call you and let you know?"

"I think that is acceptable. You will also tell me if anything happened to the car."

"Oh, nothing will happen to the car, don't you worry. I'm a careful driver, and I won't go too fast."

"Fine."

With that, he finally handed me the keys, a copy of our agreement, and bid me good luck and farewell.

The car waited for me on the street outside. I rushed in and turned on the engine. It had been a while since I drove, no less drove a stick shift. I put the car into the first gear and proceeded with the gas pedal and the car slowly moved as if it was choking. I looked around to see if anyone was watching me, but the street was empty, still waking up from the foggy dawn. To remedy the situation, I'd try to put it into the second gear but the car stopped. Instead of pushing the clutch, I had apparently pushed the brakes.

"God damn it!" I slammed the wheel as the car came to a full stop. Now I parked in the middle of the street, blocking traffic behind. A few cars already lined up behind me, waiting patiently until they didn't. The rep from the car rental place came out and stood beside the window, signaling me to open it by twirling his hand.

"Sir, you said you knew how to drive. Everything okay?" The drivers behind us honked like it was a parade.

"Yeah, yeah." I felt sweat on my face. My breathing was getting shallow and my heart was racing. I closed my eyes as if to calm down and concentrate and turned on the key in the engine again. I looked at the man and his facial expression was terrifying. "All good."

I put the car in the first gear, then the second one. I waved goodbye to the man and was on my way through the half-empty streets of Munich.

I direly needed Deutsche marks. I had a thousand dollars of cash on me I needed exchanged as soon as possible. I decided I'd park somewhere near the city center and search for a bank or a currency exchange place.

I parked near Munich Klinik Bogenhausen and walked down Montgelastrasse. I passed by the English garden that looked deserted except for a few people walking their dog. The English Garden was an enormous park where people indulged, walking naked and showing off their privates like they were Christmas decorations. I was glad to be spared of that sight. It was too cold for the brave to venture out. I got on Leopodstrasse and continued straight until I hit Marienplatz with the church, looking grand and majestic. I stared at the building in amazement, contemplating the stunning architecture with which it was designed. It stood sturdy and proud. Just a couple of blocks from the church, I found a bank with the clear sign on the building that spelled out NATIONALBANK. It would be hard to miss.

I walked in and a line of tellers were placed against the wall, but only a few were open. I approached the closest one and said good morning in English. The woman, with thick eyeglasses on, looked at me suspiciously. She looked older, and a bit rattled and irritated, as if she couldn't wait for the day to retire.

"How can I help you?" She kept the stern look on her face.

"Here to exchange dollars for marks."

"How much?"

"I have a thousand dollars." I took the money out of my jacket pocket from the inside and waved it at her.

"Okay. Give me." She extended her hand and placed it on the counter below the glass window.

Just as I handed her the money, the front door opened, the doorbell dang, and someone screamed "Einfrieren!"

What did the word mean? The woman in front of me screamed in panic and lay on the floor. I got on my toes to take a peek and she was on the floor, curled up like a turtle in its shell. The others in the bank ran like chickens with their heads cut off. And then a bullet shot was heard. I turned around and saw a man wearing all black head to toe. His robbery uniform showed only his eyes. He repeated "Einfrieren!"

I didn't know what it meant, but I assumed he meant something like, don't move or I'll shoot you. His gun was pointed directly at me, his eyes penetrating mine. I was face to face with my potential killer. While I looked at him, I noticed he was chubby, on a shorter side. His eyes were dark brown, sad looking, somewhat inquisitive. I raised my arms in surrender and waited and waited. I waited for him to shoot me, and the seconds turned into minutes, and they grew more dreadful.

In the distance, I heard the alarming sounds of police cars: nee nor, nee nor, nee nor. I couldn't tell if they were moving towards or away from us. My arms were getting tired, and I wanted to put them down to rest, but the penetrating eyes paralyzed me.

I wanted to help him. But he was too set on trying to shoot me. What was his next move? The time was passing by slowly without a resolution. I thought to myself he should shoot me now if he intended to. Get over with it. I looked around and saw no one was there, since the bank staff behind the counter dove to the ground for cover. And it was too early for customers to do their banking business. The thief must have known that.

The police cars were getting louder, closer. Just as I wanted to say something to him, to calm him into putting his pistol down, I heard the voice through a megaphone outside. Through the door, a line of police cars was parked in front of the bank. I finally felt my eyes blink, my eyelashes cutting through the air.

The voices through the megaphone were amplifying. They sounded grave and alarming.

The thief drifted the pistol toward the floor. I was no longer his target. My arms were still up in the air. The man lowered his head and he shook it with remorse. His body was convulsing uncontrollably. I wanted to approach him and find out if he was okay. But then I remembered he was the one with a gun. I tilted my head in dismay, wondering what was happening. He was crying.

A force of men came through the door and encircled the thief. "Einfrieren!"

They were cops. They all wore blue except for their black boots. A couple of them wore a cap.

The thief threw the pistol out of his hand and offered both arms to the closest cop in front of him. They pushed him down to the floor and handcuffed him. And just like that, the robbery was over. His crying continued, like a little child whose toy was confiscated.

Another cop came to me and said, "Bist du in Ordnung?"

I shook my head and said, "English."

He put his hand on my shoulder and walked me to the chairs in a corner of the bank. "Sitzen!" His words sounded like an order, so I sat down. I assumed they'd question me later on.

As I sat on the chair and watched the man taken into custody, I reflected on the trip. I could have been killed twice already—first on the plane and now in the bank. It seemed like a bad omen, a surreal bad luck. I had only hoped the things would get better, not worse.

Later, they questioned me about the incident. They found someone on the street to be an interpreter. It was a young fellow, maybe even a high school student, who possessed basic English. We somehow exchanged words, sentences, and descriptions until my testimony satisfied the cops.

I said, "Now I need my money back."

We all came up to the teller window, and the woman who took my money was still shaking visibly. Her eyes held deep fear. I said to her, "Can I have the marks? I gave you a thousand dollars earlier."

She shook her head. "No. No money. You didn't give it to me."

My brows furrowed, and I took a brief pause before I continued. "Ma'am. I gave you a thousand dollars to exchange for marks. You still have the money."

The woman looked at me, then the cop, as if to say that my claim was bogus and she was helpless in defending her position. In her fear and frenzy, she couldn't recall anything that took place minutes ago.

The cop grabbed my arm and said something to me in German. He pushed me toward the door and kept saying something, while I repeatedly insisted that they give me my money. The cop pushed me toward the door, as I screamed, "My money, my money!"

The woman at the teller window placed her hand on the mouth in disbelief and shook her head. And just like that, they kicked me out of the bank. I stood outside, penniless.

"My money, goddamn it!" I punched a fist in the air. A few passersby looked at me and made no visible reaction. They moved along to their destination, probably their workplace, or college, or a wounded lover whose heart broke the night earlier.

As I walked back to my car, furious with the bank teller and the cop, I realized I was completely broke. A thousand dollars was all I brought. With no money on me, what was I to do? My mind raced. While in Germany, I needed money for sustenance. I needed money to pay for gas and the rental car. I needed money to get a return plane ticket back to Boston. I needed money, and there was no money to be found.

Like someone just flashed a memory in front of me, I remembered Anna telling me about her cousin who lived in Munich. Rolf. That was his name. I sighed in relief that perhaps he could come to my rescue and lend me some money. I quickened my steps to the car in order to rush back to the motel and find the note Anna gave me.

The car was where I left it. I jumped in and drove back to the motel.

When I arrived, the receptionist greeted me in German and I looked at her and smiled. I had no time for pleasantries. I rushed to my room and got the note out of the duffel bag.

ROLF—ANNA'S COUSIN

I couldn't discern the numbers she wrote on the paper. God, her handwriting was awful! Was that a one or a seven?

I dialed, trying with one first, and a woman answered the phone: "Hallo?"

"Rolf?" I said as if begging for him.

"Wer ist das?"

"Rolf?" I asked again in a pleading voice.

"Nein. Das ist Matylda."

"Oh, sorry, Matylda. Have a good day!" I hung up. Then I tried with a seven.

A deep voice on the other side of the phone line vibrated through my brain.

"Hallo."

"Hey, Rolf." I tried to sound casual. And not afraid.

"Wer ist das?" If I could apply the elimination game, I'd think this meant Who is this?

"Oh. I don't speak German. Only English." Then I briefly paused. "Your cousin Anna?"

"What about her?" The man spoke perfect English, barely any accent, and I felt relieved.

"Hey, Rolf." My voice went up a few decibels and a much more cheerful mode. "Anna gave me your phone number. She and I have known each other for quite some time. A long time. But as friends. Not like... you know." I heard a clicking noise on the other side as if Rolf was tapping with something on his phone impatiently.

"I am getting ready for work. Is there something you want?"

That sounded rough. A little too direct and harsh for my taste.

"Well, I was hoping we'd meet for coffee and maybe I can tell you in person."

"Are you in trouble?"

"Trouble? Why would you think that?"

"Why?" He scoffed. "Because Americans, for whatever reason, seem to get into all kinds of trouble when they travel."

I tried to weasel out of this general and broad accusation. "Listen, Rolf. It wasn't my fault, I swear. I gave all my money to the bank teller and then she forgot. And then... and then the cop took me by the arm and walked me out of the bank, because he believed her and not me. Can you believe it? Rolf?" Then the receiver on the other end clicked and ended the call. "Rolf?" I looked at my receiver and slammed it against the phone.

"Damn it!" Just as I was feeling hopeful that Rolf was my rescue, I lost all hope. My only chance to get money was gone in an instant. What was I to do now? I pictured myself dying of starvation or getting stuck in Munich indefinitely. I placed my hands on my forehead while my head was down, looking at the floor. Time to move to Plan B.

A couple of seconds later, my phone rang.

"Hey, it's Rolf. Sorry I hung up the phone by accident. I turned around and my butt cheek caught the phone." He laughed.

"I'm glad you called back, Rolf." I sounded calmer, more hopeful.

"So? What kinda trouble are you in?"

"Well, let me tell you the story in a more composed manner." When I told him, he said,

"Holy shit. So, that's what I thought I heard. A gun shot. You know, I live across the way from the bank. The whole thing was on the news. They said the alleged thief was a Turkish immigrant. Apparently, he recently lost his job and had no money to feed his family with five kids. Five kids! Why do they bring them into this world broke as shit?"

"I don't know. Love?"

"Fuck love. If we all lived by love, a lot of us would be rich."

I could tell Rolf was a cynic, but I would not indulge in opining to him right now. I needed Rolf more than anything. He was going to be my only savior on this trip, or else I was done for.

After an awkward silence occurred, I was ready to deliver my lines.

"Listen, Rolf. I am in trouble. You are correct. Would you be willing to lend me some money and I will definitely give it back to you as soon as I'm able to?"

"Yeah, sure. How much do you need?"

"You see. I don't even know how many marks are a thousand bucks. But that's how much I need."

"That's it?" Rolf said with quick confidence. "I'm no travel expert, but you usually end up needing more, not less."

"Whatever you can do, Rolf. I'd appreciate it. I'm not much of a spender, I guess."

"Meet me in front of the bank at noon. Can you do that?"

"Yes. Yes. I can absolutely do that."

"I'll be wearing a trench coat and Dr. Martens boots."

"Great. And I'll be wearing a North Face jacket, jeans, and hiking boots."

"Of course you are."

What was that supposed to mean?

We hung up, and I looked at my watch. It was

only 9:30 a.m. I had plenty of time to lie in bed and rest up. A long day was ahead of me. Or, should I say, a long night. I lied on the bed and closed my eyes.

*Dear Lillian,*

*My father slumped into a deep depression, and he nearly lost his job. When he was depressed, he was calmer, more reserved. I hated myself for wanting him to be depressed over happy, because when he was happy, I was still sad and I couldn't bear his happiness. I could tolerate his depression a lot more. And mostly, he left me alone. Rosetta Wilson checked up on me daily and watched my father dig his hole deeper. But she wouldn't say anything as advice or consolation or a kind word. She minded her own business, and her business became me. She'd place me on her large bosom and caress my hair until the heat emitted from my head. It felt good. I wish I had told her what her hugs meant to me, but I became a bit of a mute. I spoke only when Ned or Molly were chatting me up.*

*When I turned eight, I started going to school. I was a couple of years late, so I was the oldest kid in my class. I didn't look oldest. My stature was small, and I looked malnourished. I remember that Rosetta Wilson gave me a ride to school on my first day while my father was at work. He seemed to have emotionally healed from his losses, but he never found his love for me.*

A car outside honked, and it was loud. I looked at my watch and it was 11:15 a.m. I decided I'd walk to

Nationalbank this time around. The fog had completely lifted from the rooftops and the sun shone bright, albeit not making the air warmer.

The motel lobby was empty, and I was grateful I didn't need to talk to anyone. I walked through the door and hit the shiny narrow roads of Munich.

In half an hour, I stood in front of Nationalbank. A few minutes before noon. Rolf should come by anytime. With the money. I was getting jitters as the seconds got by. I paced back and forth, back and forth until a tall and skinny man in a trench coat and Dr. Martens boots appeared from around the corner. It was Rolf. The sun shone brighter as relief washed over me.

As he came closer, I said, "Rolf."

"Hey." He wore sunglasses and I couldn't see the accurate expression on his face. He handed me an envelope and in it a bunch of paper money. "Here you go. Don't spend it all in one place."

He laughed and walked away. I watched him disappear from my sight and yelled after him, "Thank you. I owe you big time."

But he just kept walking without turning around or saying a word. The church bell called for noon. I looked up, and the sun blinded me. I moved my head back to toward the ground and the little sunspot stayed in my eye and followed me like a puppy.

## 12

Before I left Boston, Drew, my partner, asked me to call him and give him updates, but when I asked the motel receptionist how much an international call would cost, she said, "Let me check."

She had a thick book with rates for each country and city in that country and when she looked up "Boston, USA," she informed me, "Thirty-nine cents per minute."

"Thirty-nine cents?" That was way too much. I'd hoped my partner would understand that money could not be spent on these unnecessary items. What would I tell him, anyway? That I got almost killed twice, and was about to venture on one of the most bizarre and dangerous treasure hunts ever?

My plan for the day was to have lunch and head

to the Zeppelin field while it was still some daylight left in the day. I did not know what the field looked like or how long it would take to find the exact diamond spot. Once I found the spot, I had no idea how long it would take to excavate the treasure. I only hoped that things would go well. That I wouldn't get killed. I didn't want to give my life for the diamonds.

A restaurant, cozy in its size, was around the corner from the motel and I stopped by there and had a quick lunch. The windows were fogged up from the steam inside and the restaurant smelled of beef stew. Only when I entered did I realize that I was starved.

I sat a table with a white tablecloth and just as I settled in, a waiter in a black suit and white shirt came by. The menu was in German, so I simply pointed at an item—anything would do. Fifteen minutes later, the waiter came back carrying an oval plate. On it, there was a long fish—I thought it was a dorade, if not a porgy. The fish was decorated with a half lemon in its mouth, a mountain of chunks of boiled potatoes surrounded its body. On the side was a small tomato salad. All looked delicious, albeit enormous. Deep down, I was hoping for veal, but my hunger wouldn't budge. I dove right in.

When I satisfied my hunger, I was ready to head over to Nuremberg. I was nervous and excited, as I knew I was closer to the prize. I hopped in my car and pulled a map and placed it on the steering wheel. The directions were pretty clear. All I had to do was get on the highway, A9, and drive north for around hundred and seventy kilometers. That would take about two hours, maybe less, if I drove above the speed limit.

I folded the map, placed it on the passenger seat, and headed north. As I moved away from the city, the urban life dwindled. All around were fields and fields and an occasional train in a distance. The surrounding was ordinary—nothing particular to see. The signs above the highway were clear, and I made sure I didn't miss any.

My thoughts drifted away. Lillian came to mind when I least expected her to. She must have yearned for yet another letter, so I began:

*Dear Lillian,*

*When I started going to school, everyone seemed to have taken pity on me. I knew nothing about anything. Since my mother had died, the teachers considered me to be neglected. I barely spoke up, and they thought I was dumb and deaf. I eventually spat a word out of my mouth when a teacher once asked a question, and everyone looked at me in surprise and disbelief. But I developed a stutter and words didn't roll out of my tongue easily. A few of my classmates wanted to laugh, but the surprise that I spoke at all was stronger than their amusement.*

*The teacher came up to me and gave me a hand. "Come with me," she said. I didn't know where she was taking me, but I followed her, hoping she'd take me to some beautiful place with lots of toys, slides, trampolines. We walked down the school hallway; the teacher walked fast while I ran to catch up to her. We arrived at the principal's office and the teacher knocked on his door. He told her to come in and when he saw me, he made a face as if it repulsed him I was there. "What's up, Evelyn?" Evelyn was my teacher's name.*

*"He can speak!" She said.*

*"And?"*

*"He can speak, but he stutters." She looked at me and gave me a smile. I wanted to embrace her because she seemed to have cared about me. "Let me work with him. I've worked with children who stutter in the past."*

*The principal waved his hand and said, "Be my guest."*

*He turned around in his chair and lit a cigarette. He then placed his feet up on a small table across and exhaled cigarette smoke. Evelyn and I looked at each other and we both smiled.*

*Since then, she volunteered to spend time with me after school. Every single day. Sometimes even on weekends. She'd pick me up in her Ford Mustang and take me wherever she could think of. My father didn't care that I was in the hands of someone else. He didn't care that my teacher could have been a serial killer, a molester, an estranged single woman who'd turn against my father and seek custody of his child. None of that mattered to him. I didn't seem to matter. At all.*

The sign for the Nuremberg exit flashed in front of my eyes. My destination was approaching. I slowed down, so I didn't miss the field. On one side were museums and on the other was a university. The street narrowed until I arrived at a massive concrete structure that appeared to be the Zeppelin field. On the side of a long wall, there was a parking lot where I parked my Mercedes-Benz. I stayed in the car for a few minutes to study the place. No one was around.

Dusk was approaching and I could already see everything becoming a little darker and quieter. The timing was perfect.

I got out of the car and trudged toward the field. A single man was on his jog, but when he saw me, he turned left and ran toward the street.

And there I stood, in a slice of history. I once watched videos of Hitler giving his speech at this very same place. He stood on the podium, the highest point on the field, facing his loyal soldiers. Thousands upon thousands Nazi soldiers raised their right arm, palm down, and shouted, "Heil Hitler." A large flag with the swastika was hung above the field. The soldiers, all dressed in the same type of uniform, swastikas everywhere. Hitler giving his speech, brainwashing the masses. They all shouted in unison, like a well-trained bunch. Were they on drugs then? Did they know what carnage they were to cause?

And after I contemplated that slice of history and tried to imagine what it felt like to be in that place, I turned to the immediate task. The diamonds. The field was enormous. I figured it'd take me a long time to find the exact location and dig out the diamonds. I spun around like I was lost and examined all the corners of the field. With each prominent angle, I'd stop and look at the field a bit more closely.

At hundred and twenty degrees, I noticed a wooden plaque hanging on the concrete wall. It was inviting me as if it had a voice whispering, Carl, come here and check me out. I approached the wooden plaque and kneeled down to notice the ground beneath protruding a bit. There were weeds growing on the top, so it was difficult to detect at first two metal sheets lying below. I removed the dirt from the sheets. When I unearthed enough, the sheets appeared to be like a door to a tunnel, but there was no a doorknob or anything similar to pull them. I put my hand in between and tried to lift one, but it was too heavy.

It must have been well grounded with age. Forty-two years would do that.

There was simply no way I could lift the metal sheets with my bare hands. Not in a million years. I'd need to get a jack lift to aid me in the task. Which meant the day was over with the hunt, and I'd need to come back the following day with the tool. But I was convinced, almost a hundred percent sure, that below those sheets were the diamonds. I smiled as I realized my instincts never failed me. Never. Even though I could have been killed frequently during this hunt.

I placed the dirt back where it was and made it look like nothing was disturbed. I looked at the location once again and engrained it in my memory. Soon—tomorrow, most likely—I'd be rich, and all my worries would be gone. When I got ahold of the diamonds, it would be a celebratory occasion to call Drew, even though it would cost me fortune. I'd return the borrowed money to Rolf, maybe with a high interest. He was a lifesaver, after all.

Now the darkness fell upon the Zeppelin field, and I was ready to return to Munich. My course of action was to get rest for tomorrow and find an adequate tool to take with me.

As I walked toward my car, across the field, at the corner of my eye, I noticed a man with a large stature standing at the edge of the field and staring at me. He looked familiar, and I scanned my memory to recall his face. As I turned, his profile featured a small ponytail in the back and a thick moustache on his face in the front. He moved, and I recognized his walk.

It was the man who followed me when I was in Hawaii. Instead of coming to confront me, he moved away from me, with steps bold and determined. In the fear of the man, I chose neither to follow him nor to interrogate him. After all, I could be wrong. Of all men in the world, a large number must have had a ponytail, a moustache and a large stature.

When he disappeared from my sight, I quickened my pace and proceeded toward the rental car. It was still there. Untouched. I rushed to turn on the engine and made a T-turn on Zeppelinstrasse as quickly as possible. I looked in my rearview mirror and saw no one and nothing. I was all alone. My anxiety didn't let until I hit the highway. The traffic was almost non-existent, so I sped up to get to the motel as fast as I humanly could.

The more I reflected on the sight of the man, the more convinced I became it was the man from Hawaii. I suspected he was after me and the diamonds, and he was the killer Ursula had mentioned in our conversation. As I placed all the puzzles together, I got scared. I felt closer to death, and I didn't know what to do.

Somewhat rattled by the sight of the large man, I rushed to my room and picked up the phone.

The phone rang once, twice.

"Come on, answer the phone."

Just as the third ring was about to make a sound, the line was picked up, "Hallo."

"Rolf! It's me, Carl."

"Hey, buddy. You're in trouble again? Haha." His laugher was hearty and loud.

"You can say that. I need to ask you for another favor. Can you meet me in front of the church?"

"The church? Which one? There are tons here."

"You know which one I'm talking about. The big one with funky architecture."

"I'm just messing with you."

"Okay, Rolf. Good one."

"Listen. I was supposed to go out with friends tonight for a beer or two, but you can join me."

"I'd love to, but I can't." It wasn't the time to explain how much I despised alcohol. "I won't take too much of your time."

"Why can't you tell me over the phone what's up?"

"I'd love to, but the walls have ears. I'd rather see you in person."

"Fine. I'll see you in front of the church in half an hour. The church. Haha."

"Thanks, Rolf." I hung up and headed out immediately. Rolf seemed to be in a good mood, which I thought would make my request of him easier. As I walked down the street, it occurred to me I could totally trust Rolf, even though I was unclear exactly why. He seemed a bit carefree, a middle-aged guy keeping to himself, cool enough not to ask too many questions but also helpful when you needed him. Plus, Anna was our mutual connection—a lovely girl who I bet he never even harmed an ant. I should have at least asked him what cousins they were. First, second? Maternal, paternal?

I arrived at the church and the foot traffic was decently increased from the last time I was there. It was dark, and I wondered if I'd easily recognized Rolf this time. But the second after that occurred to me, Rolf was marching toward me in his trench coat and Dr. Martens boots. He waved at me, "Hey, Carl."

I was relieved to see him yet again. I smiled and wanted to give him a hug, but he extended his arm instead. "We don't hug in Germany. Sorry. I've been here too long. Have to adapt to the culture."

I was disappointed, since my hug would signify gratitude for his help. "I understand. I'm not much of a hugger either." To make myself feel better, I lied.

He stood in front of me and looked me right in the eyes. "What can I do for you now?"

"This is quite delicate, and I don't know how to say it."

"Just say it," he blurted it, almost annoyingly, to show he had not much time to spare.

"Let's move away from the people." They walked a few steps toward the church and stepped close to its wall. "Listen. I need a gun. A pistol."

Rolf's eyes widened, and he gasped. "A pistol? Did I hear that correct?"

"Yes." I wondered if I looked like a clown. First asking for money, then a pistol. "And one more thing. You need to tell me where the closest hardware store is. I need to get a jack lift and a shovel. Unless you have them and I can borrow them for a day."

"Dude. Haha. Are you starting World War III or something?" I liked his personality. He was not the type who'd be scared or repelled by my requests or demands immediately.

"Not quite. But soon, I shall be rich and you will get all your money back soon and some."

He waved his arm. "I don't give a fuck about money. Listen, I won't even ask what kinda shit your got yourself into, but I'll help you."

He was about to walk away, and I grabbed his hand. "Rolf. Why are you helping me?"

"Why not?" He walked, and I followed him. "You seem like a nice guy, plus you're sleeping with my cousin or something."

"Actually. No." I corrected him immediately.

"Anna is a lovely lady, but we have not developed a love interest for each other."

"Losers." He laughed. He turned around to look at me. "I'm just kidding."

Soon enough, we arrived at his apartment. He unlocked the front door and invited me in. His place was small, even cramped, and it smelled of old bedsheets. A few things lied on the floor like vinyl and books. Rolf didn't strike me as a person who kept his place neat and clean. But it was still decently organized for a bachelor.

"Are you married?" I asked.

"Never!"

"Why not?" My curiosity grew stronger than the situation called for.

He stopped and turned around. "Am I here to help you or answer your stupid questions?"

"Sorry. Sorry, Rolf. I was only curious. It's not important."

He took me to his bedroom, and he walked up to the bedside table, opened the upper drawer and pulled a Glock 22 and handed it to me.

"Here. I used to be a cop in the US. This one is easy to use. Have you used a gun before?"

"On several occasions." I lied to him again. I didn't know what possessed me to lie so much to Rolf. But the words came out of mouth involuntarily.

"Cool. Then you're a pro. The gun is fully loaded. As far as a shovel and whatever else you asked for, you're on your own."

"No problem. Where's the closest hardware store?"

"When you come out of my building, take a left, then two blocks down, then take a right."

I thanked Rolf profusely and I was on my way out. He slammed the door behind me without saying goodbye. Did he overextend his kindness and felt bad?

After I bought the tools I needed at the store, I headed back to the motel. I'd need another restful night in order to ready myself for tomorrow. Now I had everything: a pistol, a shovel, a jack lift, a car... and that reminded me. I stood up from the bed and dialed a number.

"Hallo."

"Yes. I need to tell someone I am going to keep my rental car one more day."

"Vot iz your name?"

"Carl. Carl Walker."

"Is the car in the same condition?"

"Sure is."

"How many more days you need?"

"I'd say one more, two tops."

"*Gut.*"

I hung up and called it a day.

**13**

---

Dear Lillian,

    *As I was getting older, I came with peace that I'd never be close to my father, that he'd never give me the love I needed growing up. If anyone got credit for showing me what love meant, besides my mother, it was Mrs. Wilson and my teacher, Evelyn. They knew my father was distant, and they sensed he wished I had not existed, so they took extra effort to be loving and kind toward me.*

    *My stutter improved. Evelyn worked with me every day. She taught me to slow down my speech when I knew I'd stutter. She taught me how to breathe while speaking. Her treatment helped. My stutter disappeared almost entirely. The only time I'd stutter occasionally was when my father and I conversed. Being around him made me nervous, since I knew he didn't want me around. But somehow, he convinced himself he didn't have a choice.*

*After my stutter disappeared, I wouldn't shut up. It was as if I had to catch up to all those unspoken years. I felt I had a lot to say all the time. Evelyn, however, questioned my stories, and she ultimately wondered if something else was wrong with me. I'd tell her what I had been up to lately or stories I shared to Ned and Molly, and she seemed skeptical. She didn't say outright she didn't believe me, but she also refused to engage when I finished telling them. That's how I knew she disapproved of my stories. Or, maybe she didn't feel comfortable hearing that I had caught a lion at the zoo, or that I stopped someone from committing suicide, or that I took a quick trip to Florida and visited Disneyland. I didn't understand why these events made her feel uneasy. Especially since in those instances, I saw myself a hero.*

I was awake, but the alarm still startled me. I looked at the clock beside me and saw it was ten in the morning. My morning was a repeat from yesterday. I got up, got dressed, and had a hearty breakfast. I had a full day ahead of me before I headed back to the Zeppelin field. My urge to walk became apparent when I paced back and forth in my room. Maybe I was too nervous. My feelings about the whole thing were uneasy. What if things didn't go well?

My chest was feeling heavy, like someone poured cement over it. I couldn't breathe. I opened up the long window and the cold air hit me. The sound of the traffic was amplified and loud. Germans seemed to enjoy honking a lot more than Americans, even when Americans rushed all the time, everywhere.

I grabbed my jacket and stormed out of the room. There was no one in the motel lobby. I stepped outside and took a couple of deep breaths. As I felt the cold air expanding my lungs, my anxiety flew away like a bird. I took a right to continue toward the city center. But something was burning inside me; my feet didn't want to move forward. My mind wanted to go back to the field, like when a killer returned to his crime scene. Though I knew this was no crime scene, part of me felt like it was. It was some sort of robbery, stealing the item I perhaps wasn't entitled to. This was no time to have self-doubt. What was wrong with me? I traveled both sides of the world with one mission in mind, and it was time to fulfill it.

I turned around and walked back to the motel. In my room, I took the duffel bag, emptied it to make room for the shovel and jack lift. I pulled out the pistol from the dresser and put it on my waist, tucked in my pants. I had seen people do this in the movies, but I didn't know if that was the right thing to do. I always wondered what would happen if a pistol went off by accident. Would the toes blow up? I didn't want to find out, so I moved the pistol into the inside pocket of my jacket. It felt safer there.

All the things I needed for my trip were in one place, and I was ready to move. The Mercedes-Benz stood where I left it. I threw the bag in the trunk and entered the car with renewed energy and vigor. The map still sat on the passenger seat, but I didn't need it. The direction of the highway was straightforward and engrained in my mind.

I drove with a high speed, eager to get to my final destination. Once I did, it was two o'clock, still early to dig. I drove around until a few blocks from the Zeppelin field, I saw a burger joint, McKay and stopped by and have a burger.

The parking lot was nearly empty. I entered the premises and two young adults greeted me. They wore yellow aprons and blue hats, and both had freckles on their face. German music was playing in the background, and it sounded like robots were fighting each other. But the place was exceptionally happy. I seemed to be the only customer, and it seemed to have cheered up the boys.

The meal tasted different from what I was used to back home. The fries were less greasy, and the burger meat tasted gourmet. Even the ketchup tasted different. After I marveled at my McKay meal, I chugged down my soda and looked at my watch. It was almost four o'clock. I thanked the boys behind the counter and walked away.

The Zeppelin field was a brief ride away. When I arrived at the parking lot, I parked and sat there staring at the side of the field. Like the day before, it was a ghost town, with nobody in sight. I wondered why the field wasn't more popular; it had lots of room to maneuver around. Did the war associations repel folks from visiting it? Slowly, the field was getting darker and more mysterious. I waited for it to fall down completely so to reduce my chance of being seen. I got out of my car and pulled the duffel bag from the trunk. I looked at my left, then my right to make sure they were no eyes on me.

The place was empty.

When I walked toward the diamond spot, all I heard was the gravel crunching under my feet. I squeezed the bag in my hand and felt my palm sweating. I walked in confidence, although my nerves were revved up.

Within a few feet, I stopped near the wooden plaque, my ultimate proof the diamonds existed. It was where I left it yesterday, untouched and waiting for me to excavate. I knelt with one leg to the ground and took the tools out of the duffel bag. The jack lift was a manual one, the smallest one I could find at the hardware store. It could barely fit in the bag. I came near the spot and took the shovel to move the dirt off the metal sheets. The ground was about four inches thick, not because someone intentionally placed it there, but because it seemed like it was accumulated over the decades. Weeds overgrew it and, like a mimicry, it was difficult to tell that anything precious was beneath.

Once the metal sheets were bare, I could finally see how brown they were from the corrosion. Each one was the rectangular shape about two by three feet in measurement. I jammed the pointed part of the lift jack underneath the metal sheet and rotated the lever. But the sheet didn't budge. The sheet was stubborn, way too stuck to the ground. I moved the lift jack to the other side and did the same, and then to yet another side until the sheet finally separated from the bottom.

Now that the sheet moved, I grabbed it with my hands and wiggled it around until it popped out completely. It was heavy, I'd say, at least fifty pounds. But the adrenaline put me in the best shape possible and kept me going. I grabbed the sheet on two long ends at the edges and, inch by inch, moved it to the side. Underneath the sheet was more dirt, with worms and maggots moving around. I took the shovel to free the space from these small creatures. Under that layer, I could see a hole, about five feet deep, and it was square and covered in cement. A rush of cold coming out of it splashed me. The hole was dark. I didn't bring the flashlight. But in the small space, I was certain it was easy to find the diamonds. Instead of pulling the other side of the sheet up, I slid down the hole and within seconds, found myself in the middle of it.

The claustrophobic feeling almost made me faint as I knelt down. I sat down and leaned against the wall. I closed my eyes to compose myself. When I placed my left hand on the ground, I felt a foreign object lying on the ground. I jerked my hand in fear it might be a dead rat or a mouse. But when I focused my eyes on it, the object was becoming more visible and clearer. It was something else, not a dead animal. It was a money sack made of burlap. I grabbed it and ran my hands over it. Inside, there were tiny little stones that danced under my hand. I put my hand in the money sack and pulled a couple of stones. On my palm were diamonds, bright and beautiful against the moonshine above. They were beautiful. Before I could yelp in joy, I realized the whole sack was full of them and I let out a scream, barely able to contain myself.

The diamonds were mine at last! I was rich. I no longer had to worry about my retirement. Onto the next prize: Lillian. She'd be a great addition to my life.

I put the diamonds back in the sack and slowly weaseled myself out of the hole. When I came out, my clothes were covered in dirt and old spider webs. In my hand were diamonds closely held next to my chest. I let out a laugh involuntarily.

The metal sheet sat on the side, and I wasn't going to put it back. The lift jack and shovel were still sitting on the ground, and I put them back in the duffel bag. As the night got cooler, I could see steam coming out of my mouth. I walked through the field toward the car, never losing a smile on my face.

Just as I approached the corner of the parking lot, I heard gravel crunching behind me. Those were not my feet or my steps. I ran toward the car without turning around and then heard a gunshot. Bang.

A coarse man's voice was heard in a short distance. "Where do you think you're going with those diamonds?"

I took a dive behind my car and positioned myself in a way the man couldn't see me. My heart was racing. I tried to think hard to get out of this situation. Ursula's warning words not to get killed rang in my mind. I closed my eyes for a second to compose myself. I put everything on the ground under the car and pulled the pistol out of my inside jacket pocket.

I peeked around the side of the car and saw a large man standing close to the Mercedes. His hair was put in a ponytail. It was the same man who had been stalking me this whole time. His stance was confident: his legs stood apart and his arms were extended toward me, holding a gun as if he was aiming.

He shot again. A bullet pierced the driver's window and penetrated through the passenger's window. Then again: bang bang. Two shots. They seemed to have hit the back of the car. It didn't occur to me then at all that I'd have a lot of explaining to do to the car rental place. I was afraid for my life. I asked him point blank, "What do you want?"

"You know what I want. Give me the diamonds and you'll be safe."

"I won't give you the diamonds. They're mine."

"Carl, hand me the diamonds. You piece of shit."

Wait, he knew my name? How did he know my name?

"Who are you?" My voice trembled from the fear of this obscurity.

"You know who I am, you idiot. We've known each other for a long time."

I peeked around the corner and looked at him again. Sure, he looked familiar, but the first time I ever saw him was in Hawaii and I couldn't put my finger on where I had seen him before, if I ever did.

"I don't know you. And you don't know me. You sound like trouble and a terrible man. And you need to leave me alone." I sounded more confident this time, but fear was still inside me. "And you can forget about the diamonds. I am in control here. I am the winner. And you are the loser. You are the one who is a piece of shit."

"If you don't give up the diamonds, I will kill you," the man said. Then he shot again: bang bang. This time, the bullets seemed to have ricocheted against the ground near me.

"You could get them yourself and you didn't. Not my problem."

"You did that for me. Hand them to me and I won't kill you."

The man was negotiating. But the diamonds were non-negotiable. After all the effort I put in, there was no way I was going to give them up so easily.

My back leaned against the car like it was glued to it. I had to think of my next move quickly, do something. I gripped the pistol tightly in my hand and turned around. He said something again, and I could sense he was getting closer to the car. I moved slowly in order to find the best position to shoot from. I heard the gravel move and the sound of it was getting closer. I stood up and fired a couple of shots in his direction.

"Shit!" He screamed. I missed him. In the corner of my eye, I saw him lying on the ground face down, trying to stand up. I stood up from the kneeling position and proceeded toward him. When I came near him, I aimed the pistol at him and fired a shot, then another one, and another one, until the blood oozed from his body. He convulsed a few times, like he was being electrocuted, then the body became motionless. His head was turned to the side. His eyes were open; his brows furrowed as if angry about soon to be dying.

I killed the man. A small blood puddle formed next to his body while I stood above him. I turned him around to examine him. He wore a suede jacket, dress-up slacks, and hiking boots on his giant feet. Up close, he looked younger than I had previously assessed him. He was not handsome, but he was rugged and manly. I placed my hand inside his pocket and pulled the wallet out. There was no money inside; only his ID, a library card, and what appears a permanent pass for a strip club located somewhere in Munich. His name was Robert Smith. Born October 21, 1951. He turned thirty-six just recently.

I threw the wallet on his deceased body. His eyes kept open, staring at the sky. I turned around and headed to the car. The Mercedes-Benz was thrashed with bullet holes and covered in dust. It looked bad —terrible—but I had a perfect cover story to tell them.

I heard the police sirens in a distance. *Nee nor, nee nor, nee nor.* Before I shifted a car gear and headed out, I touched the sack with diamonds and let out a blaring and revolting laugh. Then it hit me: it was a purely nervous laughter and, given I just killed a man, that I was in deep trouble.

# PART II

**14**

---

The tree branches swayed wildly in the wind as if they were announcing the impending storm. The wind whizzed and crackled, challenging even the strongest of trees to remain tall and intact. But inside the house was awfully quiet. A stark difference from the horrific sounds outside.

The silence was interrupted by the sound of the telephone.

*Ring ring.*

A groan.

*Ring ring.*

"Ugh."

*Ring ring.*

This was not how Oscar Gonzales wanted to be

awoken on a Sunday morning. He looked at the watch on the bedside table and saw it was eight o'clock. When the clock was moved recently to adjust for daylight savings time, his biorhythm was completely messed up. It always took so damn long to get used to the DST change. Even with the abrupt time difference, he realized it wasn't too early to receive a call, but his favorite was sleeping in on a weekend, his only chance before his week turned hectic.

Oscar lifted the receiver from the telephone and placed it on his ear, "Hello."

His voice sounded coarse and heavy.

Lauren, who woke up at the third ring, turned toward Oscar, looking dazzled by the sound. "Who is it this early?" She whispered.

A woman's voice was heard on the other side of the telephone line, but Lauren couldn't quite hear what she was saying.

Oscar placed his hand on his forehead as he listened to the woman, "A-ha... okay.... Yes. Tomorrow? Sure, I can come tomorrow."

With that, he hung up the phone and looked up at the ceiling.

Lauren came up to him for a snuggle and, still sleepy, asked, "Who was that, honey?"

"It was for Carl. Apparently, he killed a man."

While Oscar still felt sleepy, he didn't find the news striking. His voice was composed and calm, as if he was expecting similar news all along; no surprises here. "Sounds like he's in deep trouble."

**15**

———

The overhead lights were dimmed in room 212. Besides a bed in a corner, there was nothing else inside. The walls were snow white and bare. A single window on one wall let some light in. The day seemed damp and raw outside. Through the window, a view of the park was losing its vibrant colors. The trees lost their leaves, and the grass was turning dull yellow.

A woman in her early forties entered the room briefly. She came up to the window, looked through it and turned around. She looked down at the bed to check up on the man lying there. In the bed was a cover with a human head protruding under it. The woman could only see his brown hair. The man was sleeping and not moving at all. It was still early. Six in the morning. The woman came out of the room, closed the door behind her and locked it. She walked down a long hallway, which was empty. That struck the woman as unusual. An hour earlier, a janitor wiped the floors, so they looked sparkling clean. The woman walked with some hesitation, as if she was going to slip and fall down.

She walked all the way to the end of the hallway and took a left.

When she walked into a room, a man in his seventies looked up from the newspaper and under the rim of his eyeglasses looked at the woman, "How is he doing?"

"He's still sleeping."

"Ah," the man said and lifted the newspaper to continue reading. The woman sat across from the man and grabbed the ad sectional that the man had pulled from the newspaper earlier. She flipped the pages quickly without paying close attention. Her mind raced as if she wanted to say something. She crossed her right leg over the other one. When she flipped the last page, she uncrossed her leg and looked straight at the man.

"Can we talk?"

The man moved the newspaper and adjusted his eyeglasses to be closer to his eyes. He looked at the woman with concern on his face and said, "Why, of course. What's bothering you, Mary?"

"Last night, when he arrived, he said he killed a man."

The man paused and kept looking at the woman waiting to say more, but she said nothing.

"Okay," the man said.

"What if it's true?" The woman said.

"Well, is there anything else he said besides the fact he killed a man?"

"No. I'm afraid not. It was difficult to get words out of him when we asked questions." The woman ran her hand over her hair in a nervous gesture. "But he shared the description of the man he allegedly killed."

"He did?" The man asked rhetorically. "And what did he say? What did the man look like?"

"He said he was large and had a ponytail and a moustache."

"Okay."

"He also said he took his wallet out after he killed him, and he found his ID, but he wouldn't share his name."

"Hmm." The man seemed to have been thinking hard. "Have you checked the police report this morning?"

"Police report? Yes." The woman seemed dazed. "A few homicides took place in the Boston area yesterday alone. But all the men were caught and taken into custody. Unless he took part in one of them, then escaped."

"I would find that difficult to believe."

A horrific yelp erupted down the hall. Mary stood up from her seat and said, "I have to go. We will talk soon." She ran out of the room and down the hallway as fast as humanly possible.

The screams continued until they got muzzled down by a closed door.

Fifteen minutes later, Mary returned to the room looking a bit shaken. The man reading the newspaper was still sitting at the table, now staring at one spot. Now that his face was tranquil, one could see his eyes deep into his socket and wrinkles all over his face. There was a certain feeling of sadness that resonated, a certain doom that seemed to have haunted him in life. He looked up when Mary crossed the door and asked her, "Everything okay?"

"Just the usual. It never stops."

He looked at his watch on his right wrist and said, "We have time if you want to talk about the new patient."

"Sure," she said while she poured coffee in the room's kitchenette. She sat at the table across the man and took a sip of her coffee. "So, you don't believe he killed anybody?"

He looked at her and adjusted his eyeglasses, "A

few homicides in the Boston area in the last several days, all men caught and taken into custody. I'd highly doubt that it was a teamwork unless he was on a planning committee. It's usually a one-man act."

"I see." One could tell that Mary had high IQ and great instincts, but she was still inexperienced compared to the old man and had a lot more to learn. "He could have killed him a long time ago."

"No. He would have come out earlier if that's the case or not come out at all." The man seemed confident in his assertion.

"Okay. If we take that out of the equation, him killing someone, I wonder why he'd say that."

"Psychosis is quite prevalent in our patients. But the major difference is that most people with psychosis wouldn't make up inward stories. Stories about themselves."

Mary nodded her head as she listened intently. She tried to absorb the information and think of follow-up questions. "So, what do you think it is then, Doctor Farmer?"

He raised his brows and said, "I don't know, we will have to observe him, talk to him, see if we can come up with the diagnosis. Let me ask you something. How did he get admitted?"

"It's a sad story. His neighbor called the police on him and told them he was talking some crazy stuff."

"What crazy stuff?"

"He didn't really say. The police brought him here late afternoon. They seemed to think he was a danger to society."

"I see. Like I said, we will take time to observe him and come up with the next steps." He nodded his head once. "Does he have any family members we can talk to?"

"We checked, but it doesn't appear to be so. He used to be married. His wife died of cancer about a decade ago. According to the proxy, though, he has a friend we can talk to."

"Excellent. I would call that person up and summon him for questioning."

"Will do, doc."

"Oh, and what is this patient's name?"

"His name? Oh yes. His name is Carl. Carl Walker."

## 16

The mental hospital was in the heart of Boston. It stood in between tall buildings with a small park on one side. The building looked brown and square, its appearance unappealing.

It was seven in the morning and the patients were summoned at an exact time, as if they were programmed automatically. They were sent to an area where they were served breakfast. The food looked bland and unappetizing. Some patients resisted walking, and they were grabbed on each side by the hospital's personnel. The patient would try to set himself free, but the grip was strong and undeniable. He could not escape.

Second in the row was Carl Walker, the fifty-four-year-old widower. He looked thin and his head was balding. His back was hunched, and he looked much older than his age. His head was facing the floor, his eyes dropping and looking sad. When they arrived at the cafeteria, he sat down and someone placed a tray with food on the table in front of him. On the plate were scrambled eggs, in places runny not cooked enough, a piece of bread and butter and jam. A plastic fork sat next to the plate. Its edges were smooth, so it could never become a weapon. The hospital staff circled around the room, silently watching the patients. Mary stood near the door, watching Carl, refusing to take the food in front of him.

When fifteen minutes passed and Carl didn't touch his food yet, Mary approached him and asked him if he was going to eat. Without looking up, he slowly shook his head and continued staring at his plate. Mary gave a nod to his colleague on the other side of the room and took Carl by his arm. "Let's go," she said.

Carl tried to get up, but he had difficulty balancing, so he nearly fell off his chair. Mary grabbed him with both arms and helped him prop up. He stood hunched, making small steps toward the door. They went down the long hallway, passing doors on each side of the wall.

When they arrived in Suite 212, Carl's room, Mary instructed Carl to stay there. He could sit, sleep, do whatever he wanted until someone came to get him in half an hour. Carl sat down on his bed and stared down at the floor. The day was getting brighter, but the gloom was still prevalent. He looked out the window and, in the sky, he saw low white clouds mingling in the air. It was going to rain. He smelled it.

He reflected on his day earlier, just before the police came to his door. His neighbor and partner, Drew, was his enemy after all. When he arrived home from Germany, the first thing he did was dial Drew to invite him to his house. When Drew saw the diamonds, he glowed like the diamonds themselves. He put a cigarette in his mouth and lit it, but Carl didn't care this time. Drew could do whatever he desired in that moment. Even though Carl hated smoking, in his house no less, everything seemed and looked so grand, including smoking itself. Carl placed his hand on Drew's shoulder and said, "This is it, partner. We're rich."

"Yes, yes, we are." Carl smiled and wanted to give Drew a hug, but he didn't want to appear too eager.

Half an hour after Drew left with his share, someone knocked on Carl's door. He thought perhaps Drew came back to celebrate, and he'd open up a bottle of champagne to commemorate the ultimate victory. Instead, a couple of cops stood at his door and when Carl opened up the door, he said, "May I help you?"

"Are you Carl Walker?"

"Ye-ye-ye yes, I am Ca-Carl Walker." Carl felt uneasy as he stuttered. He suspected someone called them to tell them he owned diamonds, and they came to investigate. He was suddenly convinced that they found out he killed a man in Germany. The bad news traveled far and fast. The German authorities must have discovered his identity and sent the information to the USA. He decided he'd confess immediately.

"Come with us."

"Am-am-am I going to jail?" Carl wanted to understand what was happening, where he was being taken.

"No, sir, you will not jail. Do you think you have a reason to go to jail?"

"We-we-we well, I-I-I killed a man." The cops looked at each other inquisitively, and one raised a brow.

"When and where did you kill a man, sir?"

"In Germany. Just yes-yesterday."

The cops looked at each other again, and one whistled. He said to the other, "You got him?" He took him by the arm and dragged him down the hallway. Carl stopped in front of a door and stared at it. He said, "Can I, can I see Ursula?"

The cops looked at each other again and stood there as if thinking about this possibility. One gave the other a nod and gestured with his hand to do it. He knocked on the door and a woman opened it. She was in her thirties and holding a baby in her arms, sitting on her right hip. She saw the cops and gasped, "Oh my goodness! What is going on?"

"Good afternoon, ma'am. Your neighbor, Carl Walker, wants to see your mother Ursula."

"My mother? Ursula? What on earth are you talking about?"

The cops looked at each other, and one rolled his eyes. "So, she's not your mother?"

"No. There's no Ursula living here."

"I am so sorry to bother you, ma'am. Carl said he wanted to see Ursula and showed us this door. So, you're saying there's no Ursula living in this apartment?"

"Yes, that's what I'm saying. I live here with my husband and our baby." She sounded annoyed.

"Please tell us now where Ursula actually lives."

"As far as I know, there's no Ursula living in this building. And certainly, I have seen Carl around, but I have never talked to him before." She softened her tone when she saw Carl looking ill, hunched, and his eyes penetrating hers with a certain sadness. "Is he okay?"

The baby fidgeted in her arm. "He is okay. When was the last time you saw Carl, ma'am?"

She looked up at the ceiling as if she was thinking hard. Her eyes moved like the little balls in the pinball machine. She looked at the cops and said, "I think it was yesterday. He was downstairs, walking in the hallway on the ground floor. I think he had just picked up his mail, but I can't be sure." She looked at him again as if to make sure he was okay, that she wasn't getting him into any trouble. "I see him often walking around the building. He stays inside, not sure why he doesn't leave the building."

Carl remained calm and said nothing. For all he knew, he was guilty of murder and ready to be taken and put away for his misdeed.

"Okay. Well, we apologize for disturbing you, ma'am. You've been helpful." The cop raised his arm and lightly smiled. "Have a good evening."

He took Carl by the arm and walked him to the police car. Since he was caught, Carl didn't resist. He handed in himself freely, as if they were taking him to an exotic place, a spa perhaps, and he was certain he'd enjoy it. When they arrived at the hospital, the cops talked to the hospital personnel in private. They handed in Carl like he was the catch of the day. They talked among themselves and the woman talking to the cops nodded, her arms crossed. She looked tense and every once a while, she gazed at Carl who was standing among other staff tranquil and motionless. Their conversation lasted only five minutes and then the cops left. The woman came out of the room where she held the conversation and gave a nod to the staff. They grabbed him, tightening their grip and instructing him to move. Yet still, Carl didn't resist. The hospital staff stripped him nearly naked and took everything in his possession that could become a weapon or an aid to suicide. They placed his possessions in a large plastic bag and put down his name across in a black marker. He now wore a simple outfit without pockets or ropes or buttons, like he was a caveman.

The people who were directing him on what to do were rough and didn't care that they almost knocked him over. In his fragile state, Carl tried to balance, but his legs were entangled and he fell down to the floor. They picked him up by his armpits while he struggled to prop himself up. He got up and regained his balance and kept walking in between the two staff members.

As soon as he arrived in his room, he lied in bed and covered himself all the way to the top of his head. Besides terrible guilt for the murder he committed, he wasn't feeling anything else; he just wanted to sleep.

* * *

It was eight a.m. and Mary entered his room. "Hi, Carl."

He was still sitting in his bed, looking through the window. He turned around to look at her and turned back around to watch the small clouds in the sky. He thought he had seen interesting shapes; they looked like an elephant and a lion. Then he imagined what it was like to be an elephant or a lion. What was their survival game like? How did they protect their offspring? How did they hunt for food? How did they breed? Was it exhausting to be them? Were they aware of their own existence like humans were?

Lost in his thoughts, Mary had to raise his voice to get his attention. "Carl," she nearly screamed.

He turned around and widened his eyes in surprise to see her.

"Carl, can you hear me?"

He nodded.

"Good. You're coming with me now. We're going to have a chat."

A man came into the room and grabbed his arm. He told him to stand up and follow him. Carl moved gingerly, as if he was about to break into pieces. They followed Mary, who moved fast. The man pulled Carl in order to stay close to Mary, and Carl had to run. The hallway's lights were dimmed down. It seemed mysterious being filled with strange sounds coming from the rooms. They sounded like lions' roars or elephants' trumpeting. Were these humans reduced to feeling like jungle animals?

At last, they arrived in a room with a single table and three chairs on each side. The room had no windows, no smell, no dimension, no feel to it. It was bare like a poor man's soul. They seated Carl on one side of the table, and the other two occupied the other chairs. Carl fidgeted in the chair for a few seconds. The chair didn't look comfortable, and it was giving Carl muscle pain. He adjusted and returned to his tranquil state.

Mary looked at him inquisitively, as if she was studying him. She couldn't help but show empathy for the man. Her eyes looked sad as she watched him, and when she spoke up, her voice sounded soft and lovely. "Carl, we are here to better understand what prompted your admittance to the hospital. Have you been admitted to a mental institution before?"

Carl looked down and shook his head. Mary was curious about what was wrong with him. He seemed to think that he killed a man, but all the evidence suggested otherwise. There had to be a perfect story here to explain everything. With Dr. Farmer's experience and wisdom, she was sure they'd unearth the truth and come up with a right diagnosis. For now, her job was to question Carl, to get to know him better. The man sitting across from Mary was jotting notes in his notebook, transcribing their conversation. But he was also there to act as a security guy should Carl strike like lightning.

"Okay, so you haven't. Are you taking any medication?"

His head didn't move, and then he shook it.

"I see. You're not taking any medication."

"I killed a man," Carl said in outburst and cried. Tears were visible on his face, and they looked like dew on flower petals in the early morning. Mary tilted her head to the side and observed him. The man looked at her as if waiting for her to signal him to do something, but Mary shook her head. No intervention was necessary.

"Carl," she said. "Can you tell me what happened?"

"I killed a man. He followed me and I killed him."

"Why do you think he followed you?"

Carl took a pause as if he was thinking of the best way to answer her question. He said, "He wanted my treasure."

"What treasure?"

"My diamonds. I found them in the Zeppelin field. Ursula confirmed they were there."

Mary paused for a second, not sure what to say

or ask next. His story seemed implausible given, according to the cops, Ursula didn't even exist.

"How did you find this treasure?"

"I went to Hawaii and found a note that it was hidden in Germany. Then I went to Germany."

"When did all this happen, Carl?"

"I don't know. Yesterday, I think."

"What day was yesterday, Carl?"

He looked down at the floor as if he was thinking. "Sunday November 1, 1987," he finally said.

Mary and the man looked at each other in surprise that Carl had got it right. Things were getting more confusing for Mary. Carl seemed delusional, but he had his bearings. What could be wrong with this man?

"That's correct. Now, can you describe the man you killed, Carl?"

His eyes raised up to the ceiling and then dropped. "He was large. Quite large. His hair was long. But he wore a ponytail. And he had a moustache."

"Okay. And what made you kill him, Carl?"

"He... I." He stopped. "I found the diamonds in a secret spot. In the Zeppelin field. They're worth millions. The man followed me around until I found them. He said he'd kill me if I didn't hand them out."

Mary and the man next to her looked at each other again and didn't know what to make of this information. Mary kept going with her questions. "How did you find out about the secret location?"

"Drew told me. He came to me and asked me if I wanted to join him and hunt down the diamonds. He wanted my help."

"Who's Drew?"

"He's our mailman." Mary stared at him and waited for more explanation. "But he is also my neighbor. We live in the same building. As well as Ursula."

"I see. And how did Drew find out about the diamonds?"

Carl stopped to think, then he shook his head. "I don't know. He never told me."

"Where are the diamonds now, Carl?"

Carl scoffed. "I suspect that Drew called the cops on me so he could steal my portion of the diamonds. I bet he has them now."

Mary looked at him with empathetic eyes.

"I'm sorry to hear if that's the case." She pretended to believe the entire story and went along. "Well, I think we can stop here now. Thank you, Carl, for speaking with me. We will take you back to your room, where you can relax. Do you need anything?"

"Yes, can I have a book to read?"

"Let me see first," she replied to Carl. Then she turned to the man and said, "Can I see you outside?"

The man stood up from his chair and followed Mary.

"I'm on the fence giving him a book to read. On the one hand, he seems grounded right and does not seem to be harmful to himself or others. But we don't have a diagnosis for him yet and I don't know what books would be acceptable for him to read."

"I agree that it's a little risky. I say we don't give him a book. At least not until we learn more about him."

They entered the room, where Carl waited patiently. "Carl, we will take you to your room now. I am sorry, but we don't have books in the hospital to give out."

They took him by the arm on each side and walked him to his room. Carl sat down on the bed while the man was busily taking notes and Mary looked through the window. She stopped by Carl and placed her hand on his shoulder. "Dr. Farmer will see you later. Get some rest." She smiled at him and both she and the man exited the room. Carl watched the doorknob turn and heard the door lock. How long would he be admitted in this strange place?

He lied down in bed and reflected on everything that happened in the last week or two. He was wondering why his partner would turn against him or what possessed him to steal his diamonds. It was unfortunate how the situation changed so rapidly. He thought he could trust Drew, but he probably called the cops on him in order to remove Carl from the equation. How clever.

As he was thinking all this, he had a perfect view of the sky through the window. The weather was clearing up, and the sky was getting bluer. As the white clouds kept disappearing, Carl was becoming more desolate and hated the fact that there was nothing else to watch fly by his tearful and alert eyes.

**17**

———

The clock ticked four in the afternoon. Dr. Farmer had just arrived at the hospital for his shift. He moved along the hallway like a snail. He was close to retirement, but he was too attached to work, his staff, and his patients. He would have considered it a while ago, but his wife left him, as she was tired of being in a stale marriage. Dr. Farmer tried to do everything he could to appease her and make her stay, but she was solid in her decision. When she was ready to move out, she had told him she decided she'd travel the world and meet people, discover new cultures, eat new foods, work out more, enjoy life to the fullest... Apparently, she couldn't do that with him, because she always felt that he was a bit too attached to his job. He carried it with him every nanosecond of the day and she could no longer take it. She realized he was a hero to many, but he never wanted to be a hero to her. He neglected their marriage. And she finally broke down.

Dr. Farmer said to himself he'd worked a few more years, when he recovered from his wife's departure, if he ever did, and then he'd try to enjoy what little life was left for himself. Maybe he'd move to California, where the weather was pleasant most of the time. Or perhaps he'd travel around Europe. Paris, Barcelona, Berlin. He always wanted to visit those places, but he kept telling himself there would be a more opportune time later. Now that he was aged, he admitted he regretted some decisions he had made. Despite his regrets, the hospital remained his true love.

He entered the breakroom and found Mary busy around the kitchenette.

"Afternoon, young lady. Are you getting ready to finish your shift?"

"Oh hi, Dr. Farmer." She had the utmost respect for his knowledge and wisdom. "It's always good to see you before I head home."

"Well, it's always good to be seen. How are things with the patients today? Everything in order?"

"I was going to brief you on our new patient. Carl Walker. We had a talk to him this morning, and he seems pretty convinced he killed a man. He also mentioned that he found diamonds in Germany where he killed the man."

"Uh-huh. Go on." Dr. Farmer was growing curious.

"When I asked him how he found out about the diamonds, he said that his neighbor Drew told him. And that Ursula, another neighbor in their building, confirmed the location for them. But when we talked to the cops who admitted him yesterday, they said there was no Ursula living in his building."

"I see. What else might have he said?"

"He seemed completely lucid. He knew what day today was. He is emotionally fine, except for having this terrible guilt of killing a man."

"Has anyone reached out to his friend by the proxy?"

"Yes. I was told he would come visit tomorrow afternoon. It would be wonderful for both of us to be present for his visit."

"Yes. I think I can do that." As a single man, Dr. Farmer didn't have too many places to visit. His wife was always the one to organize get-togethers with people or think of places to go see. He had fewer friends as he got older and lonelier.

"Wonderful."

**18**

---

On November 2, the storm seemed vicious. The rain was falling with vengeance. The cars were moving below the speed limit on the Boston streets in order to avoid large puddles and potholes hidden beneath them. Oscar pulled into the parking lot at the hospital and before he got out of his car, he pulled an umbrella and opened it up before stepping outside. He placed both feet on the ground, closed the car door behind him, and ran toward the hospital. When he entered, he closed the umbrella and shook it, and walked up to the hospital help desk.

"Hello. I'm here to see my friend."

"Sure. What is your friend's name, sir?"

"His name is Carl Walker."

The man looked down at the sheet of paper in

front of him and seemed to look for the friend's name.

"Yes. I see his name. Is he expecting you?"

"I think so. And so is Dr. Farmer."

"Dr. Farmer!" The man's voice cheered up at the sound of the doctor's name. "What is your name, sir?"

"My name is Oscar."

The man told him to sit down in the waiting room and wait for someone to get him. Oscar didn't know what he'd expect to see upon his arrival. He was afraid he would be subjected to people who'd try to tear him apart, attack him, or, in the worst-case scenario, kill him. He twiddled his thumbs as he imagined these unfortunate scenarios, but then a woman's voice startled him. "Oscar?"

She bent down slightly in order to be on the same eye level as him.

"Yes?" He looked at the woman in front of him. She was a knockout with her long red hair and full lips.

"Hi, my name is Mary. Please follow me." Oscar stood up, happy to follow her. He checked out her rear, swinging back and forth and at that same moment, he forgot about his thoughts of losing his life here.

She ushered him into a room that seemed quite large and comfortable. He immediately noticed a view of the Boston skyline and the rain still beating down the rooftops and the ground. Close to the window was a large desk and a chair and the opposite from the desk was a couch, a bit worn out but still functional and, he imagined, handy when visitors came.

"Please sit down." Oscar said nothing and sat down as she instructed him. Dr. Farmer entered the room and found his way to the desk. He sat in the chair and looked at Oscar.

"Good afternoon. You must be Oscar. I'm Dr. Farmer."

"Hello, Dr. Farmer." Mary stood in a corner of the room with her arms crossed, trying to decide the best place to sit down. She pulled a chair from the other corner of the room, placed it near the couch, and sat down. Oscar looked at her and seemed to have been relieved by her presence.

"Thank you for coming. I understand that Carl Walker is your friend. He was admitted yesterday by two police officers who claimed that Carl's neighbor called them." Dr. Farmer paused to see if there was any reaction coming from Oscar, but Oscar remained motionless, like a statue. "His neighbor said he was saying things that made me feel very uncomfortable and suspected that Carl was a danger to society."

"Oh, no.", Oscar finally added.

"It's unclear to us what exactly happened. But we hope that you'd share anything pertinent you know about Carl so we can determine what is up, what help he might need."

"Sure. I'll be happy to share to the best of my ability. Is he okay now? Is he safe?"

"Yes, he's definitely fine. He seems to sleep a lot since he has arrived."

"You said he killed a man. Has it been confirmed?"

"He claims he killed a man in Germany. Yesterday. An unlikely scene. We checked every single airline, and they all claimed that no passenger by the name of Carl Walker traveled the past week."

Oscar gave a single nod in relief. "When I paid him a visit the other day, he told me he had just returned from Germany. I was surprised to hear it, because he can barely walk."

Dr. Farmer swirled his chair slightly before he posed a question. "How do you know Carl?"

"Carl and I grew up together in Ohio. He was our neighbor down the street."

"Ah. So, you've known him for a long time."

"You can say that. Almost all my life. Since we were small kids."

"How wonderful." Dr. Farmer almost felt nostalgic at the thought of having a lifelong friend, which he didn't. The thought of his wife leaving pained him. It was best that he focus on the topic at hand. "Do you still remember your childhood well?"

"I guess some memories are clearer than others," Oscar said.

"Yes, of course. Can you tell me a little about Carl's upbringing?"

He took a slight pause and twiddled his thumbs, a habit he developed recently.

"Carl didn't have the happiest childhood like most of us did. His mother died in a car accident when he was little—maybe four or five—and ever since, his life seemed to have gone astray."

"How so?"

"I was too small to know any difference, but I recall seeing less and less of him. All of us kids in the neighborhood played outside, but Carl stopped playing with us one day. We didn't give it much thought back then because we were just kids immersed into our game. But in the back of my mind, I wondered what happened to him."

"Did you ever try to find out?"

"Yes. I asked my mom once what was happening with Carl, but she forbade me to go visit him. She was a religious Catholic and told me once that their house was cursed. She didn't want me to bring demons home."

"Why would she say that? Do you have any sense?"

"Apparently, Carl's father neglected him. He'd lock Carl in his room often and not let him get out of the room for days unless he was going to eat. We speculated his father must have lost his mind because of his wife's death, but no one was completely sure." Oscar stopped twiddling his thumbs and grabbed his jacket and pulled it toward the floor. His nerves were getting to him, and he was getting anxious as he shared the story more. "The more my mother preached that I stay away from Carl's house, the more my curiosity grew. I couldn't help myself, so one day I headed over to his house. The front door was ajar, and I remember I was scared as hell. I was most afraid that his father would jump out of nowhere and kill me in his crazy state of mind. Or that the demons my mother was afraid of would enter my body and follow me everywhere."

Now both Mary and Dr. Farmer looked at Oscar and listened to his story, mesmerized.

"What happened next?" Dr. Farmer interjected.

"I opened the door and entered slowly, but the house was empty. I thought it was empty until I heard some voices coming out of his room."

"Voices?" Mary said. "What kind of voices?"

Oscar turned to Mary and said, "They weren't

demons. Don't worry. I don't believe in that horse-shit." He laughed nervously, but neither Dr. Farmer nor Mary flinched. "When I came close to the door of Carl's room, I heard him talking to someone, carrying a full-on conversation. But I couldn't really discern what he was saying as his voice was muffled by the door."

Now, Dr. Farmer stared at Oscar with eyes wide open.

"I couldn't tell exactly what was being said and who he was talking to, but the voice didn't stop the whole time I was there eavesdropping."

"How long were you there for?"

"Well, I ended up knocking on his door, but a strange thing happened. Next, he told me to go away, because his friends wanted to sleep and I shouldn't disturb them. I didn't know how to react to that, since Carl had no friends at that point. I was disturbed myself. Then he yelled, 'leave me alone, leave me alone, leave me alone.' Then he sobbed. I tried to open the door, but the door was locked. When I thought I had heard a car engine outside, I fled to outside the house in fear I'd be discovered."

"A-ha. Did you end up telling any adults what happened?"

"No. I wish I had, but I didn't because I was afraid my mom would punish me and not let me go out to play. She was extremely strict."

"As years went by, how did your friendship with Carl shape up?"

"Well, he got help when he started going to school. We hung out a lot more after school. Even though we're the same age, he was two years behind me in school because his father didn't care to admit him on time."

"How would you describe your friendship with Carl?"

"Strange. He always seemed to be in a la-la land, telling me all these stories. And I just couldn't believe any of it. It got much worse after his wife died of cancer about ten years ago. But I found them amusing, so I never stopped him from telling them for the same reason." He shrugged his shoulders, pleased with himself. "We remained friends because I was worried about him. I didn't know what would come out of his life given his father was such a jerk."

"What are his living conditions now? Does he live with anyone?"

Oscar scoffed as if he didn't want this question to be posed. "His condition. Ah, not the best. His apartment is a bit of a dump. He gets a pension check every month. I'm not sure who helps him with cooking or cleaning or any of that, but I stop by his place once in a while to check up on him. He sometimes gets in a certain mode when he doesn't answer his phone for days. And then I go run to see him."

"When you do, what do you find?"

"Um. It usually all seems normal when I get there. He doesn't want to be bothered. Just like that time we were kids."

Dr. Farmer nodded slightly and took a pen from his desk and twirled it in his hands. It seemed as if he already came up with some sort of conclusion about Carl, but he wasn't sure if that seemed to be the case. He looked at Oscar and asked another question. "Can you tell me a little more about his father?"

"Honestly, I know little about the man. I only heard second-hand stories about his neglect and abuse of Carl. I had seen him only on several occasions and every time, he seemed preoccupied with his thoughts. He wouldn't look at anyone, or say hi to any of his neighbors, and he wouldn't talk to anyone. He was a bit of an odd fella. I really don't know how else to describe him."

"Speaking of describing him, can you tell me what he looked like?"

"Yeah. I haven't seen him since I was a kid, so I hope my mind won't trick me. But if I recall correctly, he was quite large. Almost scary looking, given his size. He looked odd, since no one in our neighbors had the features he did. What was odd about him was that he wore a ponytail all the time and his moustache was groomed all the time. Some kids even made fun of him."

"Did you say he was a large man with a ponytail and a moustache?" Mary said.

"Yes, that's what I said." Mary quickly looked at Dr. Farmer and jotted down something on her notepad.

"But when he died in 1978, I felt like Carl was relieved. He didn't mourn his father's death that much."

"Well, this conversation has been quite helpful, Oscar." Dr. Farmer was ready to conclude the conversation. "If there's anything else you'd like to share with us before we part, please, now is your chance."

Oscar looked out the window and shook his head. "No. Not really. Do I have time to see Carl?"

Mary jumped out of her seat and said, "Oh, of course. Why don't you follow me, Mr. Gonzales?"

**19**

───────

D r. Farmer sat in his chair, looking at his desk that looked like a bomb exploded in the middle: papers were everywhere, pens, pencils, a pencil sharpener, a stapler in disarray, and somewhere in the corner was a telephone one could barely see unearth from all the things he had accumulated over the years. He was a bit of a hoarder. Once he collected evidence for his patients' illnesses, he'd hold on to it forever, but he was bad at organizing. His intern once offered to put it all together neatly, but he rejected him outright because he said he wouldn't be able to find anything anymore.

He took a notepad from his desk and looked at the jotted notes. He lifted the pages and read each page like it was a Bible. As he advanced, flipping the pages, his hand moved faster and faster until he got to the end of the pad. He unearthed the telephone under the pile of papers and picked up the receiver. "Mary? Could you please come to my office?"

A few minutes later, Mary knocked on the door and entered his office. When she saw him, she could tell that Dr. Farmer's brilliant mind was occupied with the stories about Carl Walker. She'd suspected that he could have come closer to understand the man based on just a few observations and what Oscar had told him. It was a lot. He had a lot of information at his disposal that could firm up his beliefs about who Carl Walker was.

"Sit down, Mary." She approached the couch and sat across from him.

"What's going on, Dr. Farmer? Are you okay?" She first wanted to make sure everything was fine before he shared his expert opinion.

"Yeah, I'm fine." He grunted. "Regarding Carl Walker, I have come up with a theory about our patient."

Mary sat down on the edge and nodded, eager to hear what Dr. Farmer had to say.

"Just recently, I think about five years ago, a couple of psychologists—Sheryl Wilson and Theodore Barber are their names, I believe—came up with a new diagnosis based on their research. There's something called fantasy prone personality, where the affected person daydreams most of their time and cannot tell fantasy from reality. It is an extreme case of daydreaming. According to their research, less than five percent of the population is diagnosed with it. I read up more on it, and based on everything I have learned about our patient, it just fits the bill."

Mary smiled at his brilliance yet again. "That's incredible, Dr. Farmer. I don't think I've heard of this personality trait before. You said it was a new theory, though."

"Yes, that's right. It is no surprise you haven't heard it before. From my understanding, here's how it works." He leaned forward in his chair and seemed to have concentrated. "There's something called the maladaptive daydreaming vicious cycle. There is a first step where a subject would try to escape his painful reality, which, in Carl's case, might be his childhood trauma. It could also be his current circumstances of living alone and on welfare. According to Wilson's and Barber's study, this personality trait is prevalent in people with trau-matic childhood, which Carl has."

"Yes." Mary added.

"The next step in the cycle is making up a pleasant and ideal alternate reality, which in Carl's case was befriending a mailman slash neighbor and getting ahold of alleged diamonds. This step of the cycle can take place for many hours every day, making them enter their alternate world."

"It all seems to fit within the description for Carl," Mary said.

"It does. Once the person enters their dream-like world, he or she withdraws from society, which is clear from what Oscar said. If you recall, he mentioned Carl wouldn't pick up his phone for days."

Mary nodded. "That's right."

"Because of all these steps, the real life for the person becomes even more unpleasant. In Carl's case, his neighbor calls cops on him and he ends up here, in the mental institution."

"Wow," Mary said. "So, is there a way to get out of that cycle?"

"According to my understanding, no. Once a person's life becomes even more unpleasant, he or she will resort to daydreaming again. It's a never-ending cyclic pattern just to avoid the pain. His childhood must have been terrible. And possibly his adult life, too. That's what most likely caused this personality trait."

"That's... sad," Mary said, though she knew it was not on any professional level she was saying it. "How do you explain his belief that he killed a man?"

"That... that's a bit more complicated, I believe.

My only thought is that by imagining killing a man —who had the same description as his father—he fantasized killing him for all the pain and suffering he had caused him as a child."

"Would you say he is danger to himself and society?"

Dr. Farmer leaned back in his chair and placed his hands on the armrests. "No, I don't believe so. I also believe he might have developed this trait when he was a child. It doesn't seem like he has harmed anyone, but he will get into all sorts of trouble, because he will mix his dreams with reality."

"If he's no danger to himself or society, what kinds of trouble do you mean, then?"

"He will be misunderstood, and people will think he's crazy."

"Like his neighbor did?"

"That's right," Dr. Farmer responded like a professor would when a student got an answer to his question correct.

"What's the treatment for this kind of disorder?"

"I can prescribe medication for him to keep him more grounded. But then I'm afraid another set of problems would surface, so the medication will have to be coupled with the therapy."

"What problems, doc?"

"Well." Dr. Farmer paused to think. "I'd think his childhood trauma would manifest itself in one way or another. The manifestation symptoms would need to be treated."

"What should we do, Dr. Farmer? Should we keep him a few more days to observe him with this new medication?"

Dr. Farmer looked up at the ceiling as if he was thinking, then he looked down at Mary, "You know, I think that's not a bad idea at all. Not at all. You're getting good, Mary. Very good."

Dr. Farmer smiled and winked at Mary. "It's time for Carl Walker to face reality."

**20**

---

It was November 3, and the Boston streets were getting sparser with people. Some years, winters came sooner in New England, disobeying the true calendar for their arrival. The year of 1987 was such a time. While Carl was sitting in his room and looking out the window, he felt it was going to snow soon. He had seen temperatures in the fall drop rapidly. In that moment, he felt a chill through his bones. He lied down in bed and covered himself. The ceiling above him was snow white. The recessed lights were installed instead of hanging ones. He wondered how many people would otherwise commit suicide if the hospital made that oversight. They must have thought of everything to ensure their patients were safe.

As his mind raced, Carl wondered when he

would be released from the hospital. This new habitat didn't suit him well at all. He didn't like the food; his room wasn't inviting; the people he was surrounded by seemed distant and strange. He yearned for his home, where he'd lie on his couch for hours and rest up. When Oscar visited him yesterday, he promised he would get him out as soon as possible. "They're just running some tests for a few days and then they will release you."

"I know I deserve to be here. I killed a man, Oscar."

Oscar took his hand and squeezed it tight. "You know, buddy. I'll tell you what. The man you thought you killed is still out there, alive. He's not dead."

Carl raised his head in surprise and widened his eyes. "He is not dead?"

"No. Plus, there is no evidence, if he is dead, that you killed him. You're not a suspect."

Carl felt mixed emotions about it. He wanted the man dead, but he was relieved that he wouldn't be responsible for his death.

As he reflected on Oscar's visit the day before, a funny sensation came over his body. His fingers were tingling. His hair felt like he was electric, standing up high on his head. He reached out for his chest, because his heart felt like it was about to jump out. He didn't know what was happening, but it was a physical disturbance he hadn't felt before. What was becoming of Carl?

The day before, Mary told him to take a pill that was supposed to "help him." He didn't argue and took it, even though he understood little of what it was supposed to help him with. His heart was racing, and he was afraid it'd jump out of his chest. Just as he was fighting to catch a breath, a hospital staff member entered his room on his fifteen-minute check-up.

He found Carl lying in bed, holding onto his chest, his eyes shut tight, his face looking in pain. Carl was trying to catch a breath, but he was having a hard time. The man yelled out to ask for help, and two men appeared almost immediately, as if they were waiting outside the door. Mary followed them and as she entered the room, in a panic-like voice she asked, "What's happening?"

"Seems like he's having an anxiety attack," one man said.

"Let me through." Mary cleared her way by slightly pushing the two men standing to Carl's bed. She took Carl's arm and checked his pulse. "His heart is racing. Go bring a tranquilizer."

One man ran out of the room and returned within a minute carrying a needle. He jammed the needle into Carl's arm and released its contents quickly. He pulled it out and walked away, letting Mary know it should take effect within minutes.

Sure enough, within minutes, Carl's body relaxed as if they had performed an exorcism on him and a demon left his body at last. He lied down as if he appeared to be dead. His eyes were open, his arms relaxed next to his body. Before Mary called for help, Carl turned around and smiled. "I'm feeling good. So good I can fly."

That same afternoon, Carl was summoned for a therapy. His body seemed to have found a level of peace. But inside, his emotions were murky. He was confused by everything that was happening to him, and he was trying to make sense of it. He sat in a chair and waited for his therapist to show up. The hospital was running like the military: everyone and everything was on time and a tight schedule. At exactly five p.m., Dr. Farmer walked through the door. He looked straight ahead, his brows furrowed. He approached the chair sitting across from Carl and sat down. Right behind him walked in Mary with a notepad and a pen. She enjoyed being Dr. Farmer's shadow and felt she had a lot more to learn from him.

Dr. Farmer looked at Carl in silence. He observed his features, as if trying to put the entire puzzle together. He nodded a minute later, as if he understood him more deeply. Carl's eyes looked sad and empty. The hunch on the back seemed more prominent when he slouched in his chair. Dr. Farmer couldn't help but notice how skinny he looked, almost too skinny for his height. With his face unshaved, his sporadically white beard made him look a lot older.

"Hello, Carl. I'm Dr. Farmer." Carl said nothing in return. In his confused mode, there was nothing inside. "We are here to discuss your current state of being. Our hope to release you as soon as possible. The goal is to help you go through some bottled-up emotions that have built over the years."

Carl looked at him blankly, saying nothing.

"Are you okay with that, Carl?" Dr. Farmer used his emphatic voice as if to convince Carl he was in safe hands. Carl said nothing but gestured yes with his head.

"Please, whenever you wish to talk, tell us about your childhood. Specifically, please tell us about your father and your mother. What was it like growing up?"

Carl paused and took his time to think. Silence permeated the room, with only pipes giving an occasional racket. Time became a visible item for Dr. Farmer and Mary. Minutes were passing and Carl would not speak up. His head would jerk once in a while, his mouth would move to a side. Dr. Farmer patiently waited. He felt that there was going to be a breakthrough, that Carl would see glimpses of the reality, the ultimate truth about his being. He wanted to nudge him and remind him that his sharing was crucial, but he was afraid that he would ruffle the natural sequence of events. He looked at his watch and saw that over ten minutes had already passed. He'd give him a few minutes more and then maybe he would consider saying something.

Dr. Farmer looked down at his shoes, freshly polished and barely worn. Ever since his wife left him, he'd had more time for such shenanigans. A voice caused him to raise his head, finding Carl's shoulder move in a rapid motion. Mary looked at him and shrugged his shoulders, but Dr. Farmer lifted his index finger and moved it right and left to stop her from doing anything.

Carl was doing something that he never had done before. He was sobbing hard. He felt the tears wash up his face like rain during a summer storm. His body was convulsing in the rhythm of his sobs. He let out squeals like a wounded animal. He grabbed his belly to control his hyperventilating. In that moment, he realized the childhood memories were cruel and mean and he wanted to keep them at bay. Through his tears, he looked at Dr. Farmer and said, "Please don't. Please. Please. I'm begging you. Don't."

Dr. Farmer looked at him with bewildered eyes and gestured for Mary to bring someone in.

"Please take him to his room," Dr. Farmer said.

Two men came in and took Carl by his arms on each side. Dr. Farmer and Mary stood behind, shaken by the scene. When Mary composed herself, she turned to Dr. Farmer and asked, "Now what, doc?"

"I think the session was extremely productive. I say Carl should be ready to go home in a couple of days."

"In a couple of days?" Mary sounded shocked. "Dr. Farmer, all due respect, but I think we need to keep him here indefinitely. This man does not seem well, and he needs our help."

Dr. Farmer shook his head. He looked tired. Bags under his eyes settled in permanently. He would agree with Mary and take a similar stance as he usually did throughout his career, but his own circumstances made him reevaluate things and be more lenient toward his patients.

"I know what you're saying, Mary. But I'm afraid it will take a long time for Carl to heal. The hospital can not leave him that long. We can keep him until Wednesday if that makes you happy."

Mary smiled. "I want to make sure we sort this out and help him as much as we can. Thank you, Dr. Farmer."

The next few days, Dr. Farmer tried to dig deeper, get information out of Carl, but Carl wasn't interested in speaking up. He was wasting everyone's time. He'd stare at the wall and cry, then his cries turned into sobs.

Dr. Farmer didn't know what to make of that. He reasoned that this was Carl's way of processing his past, his painful childhood. For every tear that came out, a tender memory was attached to it. One thing Dr. Farmer was sure of was that Carl Walker was not a danger to him or society. He might cruise in his dreamland every day, but he'd never intentionally harm someone.

That day of his release from the hospital finally came. Oscar received a call from Dr. Farmer the same day so he could explain Carl's disorder. Dr. Farmer determined that there was nothing more they could do for Carl. When Oscar heard, it was as if a ray of sunshine came upon him: everything became so clear. Oscar stopped by the hospital to pick up his friend. Dr. Farmer instructed both Carl and Oscar that his patient needed to keep taking medication and see a therapist twice a week. He'd set everything up for him, so things as prescribed would indeed happen.

On their way to Carl's house, he and Oscar stopped by IHOP and ordered eggs with sausage. As they sat at the table across from each other, neither one said a word. The waitress would stop by frequently to ask if they wanted a Coke refill, and they both shook their head. Carl had a poker face, as if all his feelings had exited. Oscar smiled once in a while, happy that Carl was out and found his peace.

When they arrived at Carl's building, Carl struggled to unlock the front door. The keys in his hands moved like Jell-O, and he couldn't find the one he needed to unlock the door. Oscar, standing behind him, peeked to his side to see what was going on. When he saw Carl struggling, he offered to help him.

On the keychain were three keys, and Oscar grabbed one to unlock the door. He pushed the doorknob, and the door opened. The building foyer was darker than usual; someone must have forgotten to turn on the lights in the morning. At the mailboxes stood a familiar tall silhouette and when Carl noticed it, he flinched. It was Drew, shoving up envelopes into the mailboxes. Carl stopped in the middle of the foyer and waited for Drew to do something else other than the task at hand.

After a few seconds, Carl spoke "Drew?"

Drew turned his head around and looked at Carl over his right shoulder.

"Yes?" His voice sounded annoyed and brash.

"I am disappointed in you. Very disappointed,"

Carl said. "We could have been the best partners that ever existed."

Drew raised his voice and looked at Carl with hatred in his eyes. "Get outta here, you goddamn weirdo or I'll call the cops on you again. You get it?"

Oscar took Carl by his arm and gently pulled him forward. "Let's go, Carl."

As they entered the long dark hallway, Carl's voice echoed along, "Goodbye, Drew. I won't let you into my life ever again."

When they entered Carl's apartment, everything was the way he left it. The sound of a small clock on the wall ticking filled up the room. Before Oscar bid him farewell, he sat next to him on the couch and said, "Hey listen, buddy. Take it easy now and take your meds. Okay? I'll be checking up on you every day, but make sure you answer your phone." He placed his hand on his and gave it a slight squeeze.

Carl smiled and said, "No worries, mate."

With that, Oscar stood up and walked out the door. Carl lied down on the couch, pulled a blanket over him, and closed his eyes.

# EPILOGUE

It was November 26, 1987. A Thursday like no other. It had snowed a couple of days earlier, and the Bostonians hunkered down at home, preparing for the upcoming holiday. Thanksgiving was a favorite among many, always filled with lightness, gratitude, and cheer. Turkeys were acquired, bottles of wine were bought, invitations were sent out, and tablecloths for special occasions were pulled out and placed on the table. Everything was ready for festivities.

Lillian Daisy looked in the mirror and moved her beautiful dark hair to the side. She pursed her lips, so she could put a lipstick on her full lips. Her favorite was red, and it looked superb on her. Earlier, she said she couldn't wait to celebrate the holiday, for it was her favorite. It seemed to put her in a good mood. For the occasion, she put on a black dress and a red shawl over her shoulders. On her neck sat a diamond necklace with matching earrings. She looked like a goddess, absolutely irresistible and drop-dead gorgeous.

She came down, carrying a smile on her face, the same one she wore in Hawaii. She approached the record player and placed the vinyl. The needle scratched the vinyl and gave it a pleasant crackling sound. Shortly after, jazz music filled the room. She lit two candles and placed them on the table. The smell of food came out of the kitchen and lingered everywhere in the house. Outside the window, the ocean looked mysterious as it was getting wrapped up by the darkness. The Maine coast tended to give that vibe often.

Lillian walked into the kitchen and a few minutes later, she came out carrying a big bowl of mashed potatoes. She made a few more trips, carrying out more food and placing it on the table. The food looked delicious; it would be a perfect pairing it with the red Merlot Lillian picked up on her way earlier.

The doorbell rang. Lillian approached and opened the door. There stood her friends, two couples she had known for many years. They all screamed, happy to see each other. She gave each a hug and told them to come in, to make themselves comfortable. When they sat down, they looked around as if they were looking for something. Her friend, Lauren, with a big hairdo and even bigger eyes, looked at Lillian and said, "Where is he? We're eager to meet him."

"Oh, he will be here soon," she assured them.

The front door opened and Lillian exclaimed, "Oh, here he is! He needed to make a quick stop at the grocery to get the gravy. I forgot it." She laughed.

They stood up on their feet and enthusiastically moved forward. "Hi. I'm Lauren."

"I'm Scott."

"My name is Linda."

"And I am Richard."

"Very nice to meet you all," I said.

"I'm sure Lillian mentioned, but I'm terrible with names. What's your name?"

"My name is Carl." I smiled and gave a loving look to Lillian. She smiled back as she checked out my biceps, then my rear that both looked pronounced in my outfit.

"We've heard so much about you, Carl. We can't wait to get to know you," one of them said.

"Same here," I smiled.

I grabbed a bottle of wine and poured it into six

stem glasses. I did not drink alcohol, but I decided this was a special occasion. Next to me stood Lillian, and the world seemed to come together at last. If I made any important decisions, finding her was the best one. And it felt right. For I, Carl Walker, was the commander of my destiny.

# THANK YOU!

I sincerely thank you for reading this book!

Please consider leaving a review, even if it's only a sentence, checking out my other books, and subscribing to my website. I'm also happy to answer any questions you may have, so do please get in touch with me via my website:

https://nadijamujagic.com

ALSO BY NADIJA MUJAGIC

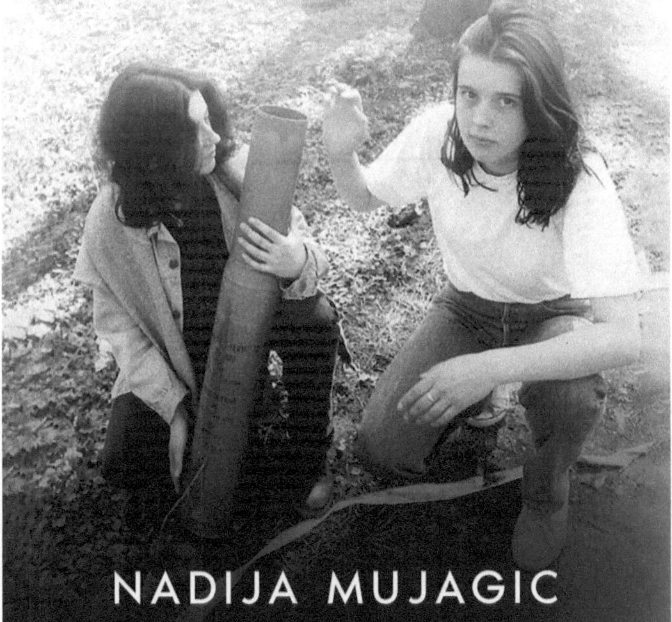

# NADIJA MUJAGIC

After surviving the
Bosnian War and moving
to America, she was
determined to succeed
as never before.

# Immigrated

A MEMOIR

# TILL A BETTER WORLD

A NOVEL

## Nadija Mujagic